Excerpt from One Horse Open Sleigh Race

She transferred her gaze from his handsome, angry face to the enormous black horse standing nearby. The thought of poor Hamish running under its powerful legs nearly started Amanda trembling. "I thank you for that," she said.

"Is that supposed to be an apology?" He returned to the horse and crammed the hat into the saddlebag.

Irritation inched its way over Amanda's skin. "No, but I'll offer you one. I'm sorry Hamish startled your horse and made you fall."

"And is that what I'm supposed to tell my valet when he sees my coat? It at least might be salvageable." The man swung into the saddle, pushed a strand of dark hair out of his eyes and peered down at Amanda.

One Horse Open Sleigh Race

Karen Hall

ISBN-13: 978-1492772743

ISBN-10: 1492772747

Chapter One

"Reverend Smythe is dead?" Cameron, "Cam" Hunt, the ninth Earl of St. Cloud stared across the desk at his bailiff. "Good God, Arwine. It's two weeks until Advent. Where will I find another rector on such short notice?"

"The late Mister Smythe was never known for his sense of timing," agreed Thomas Arwine. His weather-beaten features settled into a frown. "Rather bad manners, if you ask me."

"Not to mention, extremely poor taste," Cam growled. "What killed him?"

Arwine cleared his throat. "It would seem the late Mister Percival Smythe died yesterday evening after enjoying a rather large bottle of brandy given to him by a parishioner."

"You mean he drank himself to death?" Cam muttered another oath more appropriate for a gaming hell than a London townhouse library, squashed his unfinished letter and tossed it into a nearby basket.

"So it would seem, my lord," Arwine said. "I had George ready the carriage first thing this morning so I could come and tell you. We left as soon he could see the road."

"Thank you for that," Cam said. He rose and crossed the room to stand by the fireplace. "Has anything else happened in my little corner of Surrey, Arwine? Please tell me everything else is well in Huntingdown and at Heart's Ease."

At the mention of the St. Cloud country-seat, Arwine stood a little straighter. "Everything at Heart's Ease is as you would have it, my lord. And naught else is amiss in Huntingdon."

"Thank God for that." Cam released a sigh or relief. "When is Smythe's funeral service?"

"Tomorrow at noon in Guildford, my lord."

"Very well. We'll leave as soon as I can have Higgens pack my things and we've eaten. Go see if George needs any help switching out the horses."

Arwine bowed and left. When the door clicked close behind him, Cam walked over to the bow window and stared into the street. Blazes, he did not need this. The Little Season was almost finished, but still made much demand on his time. The invitations to teas, balls and weekend house parties were piled in a dangerously towering abundance on his desk. Such was the fate of a bachelor earl who was not only immensely rich but regarded as very handsome, and therefore in need of a wife.

And according to the promise he made to his late father, Cam would follow the St. Cloud family tradition and be married—or at the very least engaged—by the time he turned thirty. As the thirtieth anniversary of his entry into the world was this approaching New Year's Day, Cam's time was running out. He needed to find a candidate for his wife, and soon.

To be sure, there were eligibles by the score. Cam knew this because he met every last preening, simpering, giggling, eyelash fluttering one of them. All eager to know his taste in music, books and architecture, so they might comment on it. Heavens, the conversations he endured. Was there not a single woman of his class in London who could talk without giggling?

To become the Countess of St. Cloud would be a tremendous challenge and not a role just anyone could fill. Centuries of tradition preceded it, and Cam was hard pressed to think of a woman of his acquaintance who could match his late mother's impeccable style. It would be easier to find a new rector for All Souls than to find a wife.

Like his forefathers, Cam firmly believed in following family tradition. The only time he broke with it after he became St. Cloud at twenty-two was to allow his younger brothers to marry before he did—and then only because they both threatened to elope to Gretna Greene or some such place if he did not allow them to announce the banns. Only his sister Perdita, scheduled to come out next spring, remained. If he were lucky, his new countess could present Perdita at Court. That is, if he found her. Despite his efforts, he remained a bachelor.

There *might* be a candidate. The Honorable Lucy Guest, daughter of Viscount Pembroke, did not giggle or simper or bat her eyelashes. Her father's estate was near Cam's in Huntingdown and the Pembrokes, like the St. Clouds, always spent Christmas there. Lucy was pretty, intelligent and like Cam, a firm believer in family tradition. Cam's father even suggested he consider such an alliance when Lucy came of age three years ago.

But instead of making her bow like all the other eighteen-year-olds that Season, Lucy insisted on attending The Brentwood Academy for Young Ladies, an exclusive finishing school in Darbyshire with a program that lasted three years.

And since Lucy always got what she wanted, her parents gave in to her request. This past spring, Lucy's presentation at Court and introduction into Society had been declared a triumph and Lucy hailed as the "most brilliant of diamonds."

In private, Cam gave Lucy full points for her insistence that she attend Brentwood. Asking an eighteen-year-old to step into his late mother's shoes would have been impractical at the least and an unkindness at the very worst.

But now the girl Cam knew transformed into a polished, sophisticated young woman, equal to any challenge an Earl's wife might face. Never one to rush into a hasty decision, particularly in something as important as marriage, Cam watched and waited for Lucy to enjoy her first Season. He wasn't so proud as to think he might be her only choice. But claims of broken hearts and shattered souls at her refusals for men to even call on her, filled half the London gossip and scandal sheets. This led Cameron to think that perhaps she might be waiting for his proposal. And the joining of their two houses would bring honor to both of them. His destiny was clear. Cam nodded at his reflection in the window's glass. He would approach Pembroke this Christmastide and ask for Lucy's hand in marriage.

Of course, he would also have to wait for the arrival of Lucy's beloved great Aunt Adelaide Cheswick, Dowager Duchess of Clairfield and a dragon if there ever was one, especially where it concerned Lucy. She made the patronesses of Almack's look like a group of schoolgirls. Aunt Adelaide liked to travel and was reported to be somewhere near India.

Of Lucy's acceptance, Cam had little doubt. They liked each other well enough and after all, what girl wouldn't want to marry a rich, handsome earl in need of a wife?

Now all he needed to do was find a new rector for All Souls.

****

Two weeks later.

"Whoa!" The post driver pulled the horses to a stop. The wheels splashed through a row of puddles, which almost made twins Amanda and Stephen Fleming tumble from their seats. Hamish, their Scottish terrier, wasn't so lucky and the dog slid from beside Amanda to the floor, where he landed with a decided thump.

"Good heavens!" Stephen proclaimed, using the strongest oath he possessed. "Why did we stop?"

"I haven't a clue, brother." Amanda helped Hamish back onto the seat. She peered out the window into the mist that swirled around the yard, and said, "Surely this isn't Huntingdown?"

"I don't think so." Stephen opened the window and called, "Driver! Why are we stopping?"

The other door jerked open in answer and the grizzled driver peered inside, his eyebrows drawn together to match his ferocious frown. "'Tis the fog, sir. I carn't see much ahead. We best wait a bit 'til it clears up. And t'will be a good a place as any to stretch yer legs and have a sup of some of the finest cider in these parts. But don't ye worry none pastor, I'll have ye and yer sister at the rectory by suppertime."

He didn't wait for their answer, but turned and lumbered toward the two story stone building. Light blazed from the mullioned windows and delicious odors wafted out from the open door. The coachman slammed it behind him, and the twins traded glances. Amanda spoke first.

7

"I suppose we don't have any choice except to wait until he satisfies his thirst," she said. "But I don't think the fog is that bad."

"Neither do I, but I'm not driving us," Stephen said. "And I would appreciate something cold and sweet to drink, wouldn't you?"

"I'd rather have a cup of tea." Amanda secured Hamish's leash to his collar. "And I would enjoy the chance to stretch my legs a bit."

"So would Hamish, no doubt." Stephen alighted from the hired coach and then helped her down. Hamish bounded after them, nose already to the ground, his tail wagging furiously.

"I just hope there are no rabbits about." Amanda tightened her grip on the leash. "The last time he spotted one, he dragged me through a bunch of thistles."

"Do you suppose everything will work out for us? The living at Huntingdown, I mean?"

Amanda blinked at her brother's sudden question. "Of course, it will. Why wouldn't it?"

"It's my first real living, and such a magnificent one too," Stephen said. A solemn light entered his green eyes. "A partially furnished house with a staff of five, only four miles from Hounslow and ten miles from London. And such a generous salary. Why choose me of all people? Perhaps I should have accepted Master Phillip's offer of that teaching position at Balliol at Oxford."

"Because you're a wonderful minister and scholar," Amanda praised, tweaking his woolen scarf into place. "It was high time you were offered a position worthy of your talents. Saint. Barnabas almost fell down around us, the rectory was always cold, and the salary barely enough to make do. Not to mention, a grumpy congregation and a vestry determined not to change anything, including making improvements to the church. Your position at Church of the Good Shepard was almost as bad."

"I mean, besides all that," Stephen countered, and they shared a laugh. "You're right of course, Mandy. If anything, the other churches were a good training experience. I wonder what kind of man the Earl of St. Cloud is? From Master Phillip's description, he's not much older than I am, and already an Earl. He must be imposing, indeed."

"As long as the rectory is warm and the church roof doesn't leak, St. Cloud could be Napoleon and I wouldn't mind," Amanda said. "Perhaps he——ouch! Hamish, stop!"

Hamish's loud bark and brisk tug at his leash signified his impatience with their conversation and Stephen laughed again. "You better let him go sniff the bushes," he advised. "I'll go ahead and order your tea. Watch out for those puddles over there."

He headed toward the inn with his long stride and Amanda let Hamish lead her toward a grove of trees. The mist thickened around them and stepping carefully, she followed Hamish into the grove and undid his leash. Bounding ahead, the little Scottie moved from tree to tree, where he scratched and growled as he made his exploration. A breeze ruffled the treetops, and shivering, Amanda pulled her scarf more tightly around her head.

"Everything at Huntingdown will be just fine," she said, more to herself than to Hamish. "If I can just learn to mind my tongue and not always say what I think. Stephen doesn't need trouble with his new parish because of *me*."

Because even though he had never said so, Amanda suspected Stephen's leaving his two previous assignments—St. Barnabas in Sudburough, Northamptonshire and Church of the Good Shepherd near the coast in Maumsby, Kent—was because of her. Amanda struggled to rein in her frustration at the churches' entrenched way of doing things, and refusal to even consider change. But eventually her outspokenness always got the better of her. She'd never found a way to fit into village life or felt at home in either place. Her coldly polite and regular battles with the Ladies' Auxiliary or the Altar Guild at both churches only made things worse. Stephen, bless his heart, never said a word of reproach.

"It just wasn't a good fit for us, Mandy," he said after he'd decided to leave Maumsby. "We'll find a place soon."

"This time, I'll do better," Amanda vowed. "I'll be sweet, discreet and a pleasure to meet. Hamish, you've left your mark on enough trees. Let's go have tea."

The Scottie scampered back and she put on the leash again before heading back toward the yard. The breeze picked up and Amanda shivered again as her companion made one last stop. "Hurry up, Hamish," she scolded. "I'm going to freeze to the ground in another— Hamish, come back here!"

The sudden appearance of a large rabbit in their path made the Scottie hurtle forward with a throated bark. The leash snapped from Amanda's hand. She dashed after him into the yard just as a rider on a large black horse galloped out of the mists. Hamish's pursuit of the rabbit brought him within inches of the horse's hooves. Shock froze the scream in Amanda's throat as the great animal reared back with such force, that its rider fell from the saddle into a large puddle, sending its muddy contents upward like a renegade fountain. His hat landed beside him, and a vigorous oath proved that the rider was still among the living.

"Hamish!" Amanda shouted in relief. "Come here!"

Hamish scampered back and with a practiced leap, hurled himself into her arms as the man picked up his hat, got to his feet and brushed a strand of black hair out of his eyes. With a barely audible oath, he stumbled back to his horse and turned to face her. Eyes as dark blue as a starless night, fixed on Amanda's face and she was grateful to have Hamish clasped against her body. The scowling man who stood opposite her looked very angry indeed. She tried to keep her voice from wobbling, and ventured to ask, "Are you all right?"

"No, thanks to you and your dog." The man held one foot slightly off the ground, and tried to brush his coat free of mud. His scowl deepened as he stared at his saturated glove. "Why in blazes did he charge at me like that?"

"He saw a rabbit," Amanda explained, trying to keep the heat from rising to her face. It certainly wasn't from his language. A clergyman's daughter certainly heard worse. And where in the world was Stephen? She turned her head toward the inn, and heard laughter and loud singing. She hoped their driver wasn't drinking hard cider. The Lord only knew when they might arrive at the rectory.

"And you couldn't keep better control of him?" The man shook his hat, which sent a shower of muddied droplets to the ground. Limping forward, he held it out for Amanda's inspection and she swallowed the lump in her throat. Even without his boots, he would be taller than the average man.

"This is ruined, by the way," his baritone voice accused. "You're lucky that Socrates didn't run your dog down."

She transferred her gaze from his handsome, angry face to the enormous black horse that stood nearby. The thought of poor Hamish running under its powerful legs nearly made Amanda tremble. "I thank you for that," she said.

"Is that supposed to be an apology?" He returned to the horse and crammed the hat into the saddlebag.

Irritation inched its way over Amanda's skin. "No, but I'll offer you one. I'm sorry Hamish startled your horse and made you fall."

"And is that what I'm supposed to tell my valet when he sees my coat? It at least might be salvageable." The man swung into the saddle, pushed a strand of dark hair out of his eyes and peered down at Amanda.

"Surely valets know how to do such things," Amanda retorted. "Or perhaps if you had better control of Socrates, you wouldn't fall."

His eyes narrowed and his lips parted as though prepared to deliver a stinging retort. Instead, he gave a low, sharp, whistle, and Socrates broke into a trot, then a canter and finally a gallop. Amanda watched horse and rider disappear into the swirling mist before she put Hamish down.

"Wretched man," she muttered. "I hope his valet is up half the night, scrubbing that coat. Good boy, Hamish."

"What's he done now?" Stephen asked, appearing at her side. He handed her a cup of steaming tea and took Hamish's leash.

"Nothing," Amanda said quickly. Not the best thing to lie to one's clergyman brother, but the *last* thing they needed was trouble with a local—one obviously very high in the instep—before they even arrived at the rectory. She would tell him about it before he made his calls.

She drained the cup, gave it back to him and took Hamish in her arms "Let's go, brother. I want to see the rectory before it's too dark."

And before I cause any more trouble.

Chapter Two

"Did Higgens ever get your coat clean?"

Cam shifted on the seat of his smallest carriage—the one he used to visit their tenants and local gentry on less formal occasions—and raised an eyebrow at Perdita's question. Outside, a fine snow fell, and added another layer to the already covered ground. "And how did you know my coat needed to be cleaned?"

Beside him, his sister's dark blue eyes twinkled in a way not quite appropriate for a young lady who just completed the finest finishing school in Middlesex. "I heard him tell Flora about it last night after we came home. He said both your coat and gloves were *absolutely* covered in mud. Did you *really* fall off Socrates?"

Your maid and my valet should have better things to do than discuss my wardrobe problem. "Yes," Cam admitted reluctantly. "A rabbit startled him."

"Poor brother," Perdita said, but her widening smile belied her sympathetic words. "To think of the Earl of St. Cloud on the ground, soaked in mud because of a fierce, wild rabbit! And your poor ankle too. Does it still hurt?"

"No," Cam growled. It was bad enough to wait until the mud dried on his coat before Higgens could take a good stiff brush to it. The gloves were given up to the trash, and pronounced a "lost cause" by a mournful Higgens. And despite several soakings, his ankle continued to throb. If he moved slowly, his limp was hardly noticeable.

Worse still, he could not shake the memory of a tall, slender woman stepping out of the mist, strands of gossamer blonde hair slipping from under her scarf, her green eyes wide with shock. She called up an image of a wood sprite, wild and fey, ready to capture and drag him back into a netherworld. She haunted his sleep for the past two nights, making him impatient and out of sorts. Good thing she was long gone. "Did you enjoy your morning ride, Perdita?"

"Yes, and you'll never guess what I saw. They've hung the garlands on the gates at All Souls. It's beautiful. And there are two wreaths on the doors, covered in red and silver ribbons and tiny bells. They're simply *huge!*"

"Very nice," Cam replied resignedly. In spite of her first rate education, and lessons in lady-like deportment, Perdita's natural enthusiasm for life simply could not be curbed. It bubbled from her like the best of champagnes and almost everything excited her. Her husband—when Cam found one he approved of—would have a hard time reigning in her exuberance.

But it was that same innocent exuberance that made his only sister adored by the entire staff at Heart's Ease. Everyone, from Oakley, the St. Clouds' venerable butler, to Cassie the little kitchen maid, loved her without hesitation. And because Perdita loved them with an equal fervor, they spoiled her without reservation. But despite that, Perdita remained as unaffected as if she was a farmer's daughter instead of an heiress.

"Have you met the new rector yet?" she asked.

"He called on me two days ago, just before I came to fetch you, to thank me for giving him the living," Cam said. "That's why we are going to the rectory now for tea."

"What's he like?"

"What do you mean, 'what is he like'?"

Perdita gave him a gentle dig in the ribs with her elbow. "Don't be perverse," she scolded. "Is he young, old, thin or fat, handsome or ugly?"

"Hmm." Cam pretended to frown in concentration. "He's nine feet tall, has two heads—"

"Cam."

"—weighs several hundred pounds, has a wart in the center of his head, and has a sister." At Perdita's frown, he amended, "Well, perhaps not as bad as all that; I'll let you make your own judgment. He has excellent manners, and supposedly likes to give short, to-the-point, sermons."

Perdita's sudden laughter filled the carriage. "Well, at least that's better than the late, unlamented roly-poly Percy Smythe. Lord, what a mutton-headed mushroom he was. His sermons were such snoozers they would put me into a right old dudgeon. Most definitely not all the crack."

"Perdita!" Cam's voice rose. "Where did you learn language like that?"

"From you, Allister and Richard." Perdita's eyes widened. "You always talk that way about someone you don't like."

"It's not language for a young lady," Cam scolded.

"Then perhaps you shouldn't talk where I can hear you," she countered primly.

"You mean where you can eavesdrop," Cam said, keeping his stern tone. "We'll discuss your linguistic habits later."

"Oh, very well." Perdita allowed him the point. "You've not mentioned if Mister Fleming is a married gentleman or not."

"He's a bachelor," Cam said. "That's why his sister came with him to help run the household."

"A sister?" Perdita leaned forward. "Really? Did she come with him when she called?"

"No. She was helping Mrs. Crawford re-organize the kitchen and going over the household linens with Alice."

"Oh." Perdita's shoulders slumped a bit. "Then you don't know if they're the same age or what she looks like."

"Does that matter?" Cam asked.

"I hoped to meet someone new and exciting this Christmas season," Perdita complained, "or it will be the same dull people as always."

"Hush," Cam warned. "We're here. You'll have enough excitement getting ready for your debut next year to last a lifetime."

The carriage stopped in front of a brick two-story house next to All Souls Church and they stepped out. Just as Perdita described, two enormous green wreaths hung on the church's double doors and someone wove ivy around the iron fence. Smoke wafted from the rectory's chimney, and the steps that led to the porch gleamed— proof of a fresh scrubbing.

The front door opened before Cam could raise his fist to knock. Alice, the parlor maid, ushered them inside and curtsied. "Good morning, my lord. Good morning, Lady Perdita."

"Good morning, Alice," Cam said. "I presume our hosts have settled in comfortably?"

Alice gave a quick nod. "Yes, my lord. But heaven help us, all them books! And that Sco—"

"My lord St. Cloud."

A tall, slender, blond man came loping across the foyer. He stopped before them and bowed. "A pleasure to see you again, my lord."

"Perdita, this is Mr. Stephen Fleming, the new rector of All Souls," Cam said. "Mr. Fleming, my sister, Lady Perdita Hunt."

19

The clergyman gave her a dazzling smile and bowed again. "I'm delighted to meet you, Lady Perdita. My sister Amanda looks forward to meeting you as well."

Perdita beamed and offered him her hand. "How do you do, Mr. Fleming? I hope the rectory is to your liking?"

"It's wonderful," he said. "Such spacious rooms, and chimneys that don't smoke, which is a blessing in itself. The library is big enough for all my books, and I imagine in the spring the garden will look splendid. And thank you, my lord, for providing a horse and covered wagon too so I might do my pastoral visits no matter the weather."

"And the staff?" Cam asked. "Are they giving satisfaction?"

Fleming sighed happily and took Perdita's arm. "To tell you the truth, my lord, this is the first position I've had that came with a staff of five. Amanda and I shall be quite spoiled by having a cook, housekeeper, two maids and male servant. Amanda won't know what to do with all the extra time she will have. Amanda? Our guests are here."

He led Perdita across the foyer, and Cam followed them into the sunny room. Then shock rooted him to the spot, making further movement impossible, as the cause of his sleeplessness—not to mention his ruined gloves and sprained ankle—rose from a chintz-covered loveseat near the fireplace. The sprite stared at him, face flushed, her eyes grown to the size of saucers while her hands quickly locked together and she stood as immobile as he.

Barking issued from a large basket in the corner as its occupant charged forward, tail bristling. The growling Scottie quivered before them, his black eyes fixed on Cam, who uneasily remembered a Scottish friend at school warning him that Scots had notoriously long memories. Obviously that applied to their dogs as well.

"Hamish, stop," Fleming ordered, and thankfully, the dog stilled. He trotted back to the sprite and sat, but continued to stare at Cam, as if deciding which part to taste first.

"I beg your pardon, my lord," Fleming said "He's really very friendly."

"Of course he is!" Perdita cried. Kneeling, she coaxed, "Come, Hamish. Can't we be friends?"

The little dog trotted to her, and Perdita scooped him into her arms and stood. Hamish licked her face, his tail wagging furiously.

"There, you see, brother?" Perdita scratched Hamish behind the ears. "He's a sweetheart."

"I'll remember that," Cam said, watching the sprite. The blush faded from her face, but her still tightly clasped hands suggested her earlier agitation remained.

"Well, I'm glad that's settled," Fleming said. "Amanda, this is our benefactor, Cameron Hunt, the Earl of St. Cloud and his sister Lady Perdita Hunt. My lord, Lady Perdita, this is my sister, Amanda.

Miss Fleming preformed a graceful curtsy. "My lord St. Cloud. Lady Perdita. Thank you for offering Stephen the living, my lord. I have no doubt we'll be most happy here."

"You didn't tell me he had a *twin* sister, Cam." Perdita scolded.

"He didn't mention it," Cam said, his gaze never leaving Miss Fleming's face. "Or that they had a dog."

"Didn't I?" Stephen frowned in thought. "Odd. Well, never mind. As you can see—"he gestured at a food-laden table. "Mrs. Crawford prepared a late morning tea for us. Has she always cooked at the rectory?"

"For years," Cam said. "All of your current staff have, and there has never been any complaint. But do let me know if you find there is anything else you might need or want."

"Well, as usual at this time of day, I'm famished," Stephen declared, rubbing his hands together. "Amanda will do the honors, won't you sister?"

"Of course." Miss Fleming said, and Cam thought he heard a faint tremor in her voice. "Won't you please be seated?"

"You're limping, my lord," Stephen said. "I hope you didn't fall on your way here."

"A rabbit frightened Cam's horse the other day and he fell off," Lady Perdita explained as she sat. "Poor brother."

"I hope your horse sustained no injury, Lord Hunt?" Miss Fleming asked smoothly as she filled the cups with tea. "Sugar? Lemon? Milk?"

"None, thank you, Miss Fleming." Cam managed to keep his tone steady. "And my ankle, while still sprained, is healing quite nicely."

"I'm so glad." A smile hovered around his hostess's lips as she gave him his cup. "Rabbits can be such a nuisance, can they not?"

She finished serving the others and sat in the chair next to Perdita, who fed Hamish tiny pieces of a scone. After asking a number of questions about village matters, Fleming gave his sister his cup and sat forward.

"Someone told me there's a sleigh race the day before Christmas Eve," he said. "Can you tell me about that, my lord?"

Cam shrugged slightly. "The race is the last event in a series of holiday activities held the week before Christmas. Traditionally, my family holds a ball the night before the race. The race is open to anyone in the village if they have the driving skills. The contestants are required to use a one horse sleigh, such as a Tilbury or a Sulky to race on a back stretch of property covering two miles at Heart's Ease."

"Cam and my other brothers have won many times over the years," Perdita said proudly. "They're all excellent whips."

"Be honest, Perdita," St. Cloud cautioned. "We've not won for three years."

"Well, now that I'm home for good, you'll just have to try harder." Perdita handed her cup back to Miss Fleming. "Do you race, Mr. Fleming?"

"I've been known to go in for neck or nothing in my time," the rector said cheerfully. "A benefit of growing up in rural Hampshire, I suppose. Amanda rides too. Did you pack your riding habit, sister?"

"Yes, but as we only have the horse for you to do your visits, I won't be doing much riding here," Miss Fleming sighed. .

"Oh, we have any number of horses you could borrow," Perdita said. "We must go sometime. You can choose from our stables, can't she, Cam?"

"If she wants." Cam directed his gaze at Miss Fleming. A faint blush spread across her cheeks and her fingers played with the pearls around her neck. Cam thought she exchanged a glance with her brother and wondered if it were some kind of signal between them.

"Well, if the race is open to everyone, I think I'd like to try my hand at it," Fleming said cheerfully. "Unless there's a restriction for a member of the clergy to do so."

"None that I'm aware of, Mr. Fleming. We'd be happy to have you enter." Cam finished his tea and set his cup on the table. "Have you spoken to the choirmaster about Perdita singing this Advent and Christmas season?"

"I have indeed," Mr. Fleming affirmed with a nod. "He is full of nothing but praise for her musical talents. I do hope we can count on you to join the choir this Christmas season, Lady Perdita."

"I would like nothing better," she said. "Do you sing or play the pianoforte, Miss Fleming?"

"Not very well," Miss Fleming said. "But I am most talented at turning pages for others."

"You can certainly say that," Mr. Fleming agreed, provoking a laugh from Perdita. But recalling his ruined gloves and stained greatcoat kept Cam from joining their mirth. "A talent you are no doubt called on to use on any number of occasions," he said dryly.

Miss Fleming raised her chin as if issuing a silent challenge. "I'll be happy to demonstrate at this Sunday's service if help is needed.. That is if your ankle will allow you to attend."

"Speaking of music, Lady Perdita needs to practice for her lesson this afternoon." Cam rose and bowed. "Thank you for your invitation and hospitality, Mr. Fleming. Miss Fleming. Come, Perdita."

With a sigh, Perdita put a protesting Hamish on the floor. "I hope you will call on me soon, Miss Fleming," she said.

"I would like that," Miss Fleming said, getting to her feet. That is if my lord St. Cloud will permit me to do so.".

"Of course he will!" Perdita exclaimed before Cam could answer. "I'll send a note 'round." Excitement lit up her face. "You can turn pages while I practice my singing and I can show you Heart's Ease and we can go riding—"

"Come, Perdita," Cam ordered again. "We've intruded on the Flemings's hospitality enough for one day."

He headed for the hallway, trying not to let his limp slow his progress. But Perdita, as if to vex him, took her time in saying goodbye to the Flemings. At the door, Cam turned to see her bend down to scratch Hamish's ears. "I'm very glad to have met you, Sir Hamish," she said. "You may come and visit Heart's Ease as well."

The little dog offered her his paw in farewell, but his black eyes were only for Cam. They studied him for a long moment, then one slowly and deliberately winked. Behind him, Miss Fleming watched, her own eyes bright with unspoken mischief, and a strange apprehension set Cam's heart pounding at a curiously rapid rate.

"Come Perdita," he called again and this time his sister obeyed. Once they were inside the safety of their carriage and on the way back to Heart's Ease, Perdita squeezed his hand. "I say, Cam. Aren't the Flemings the nicest people? Really bang up to the knocker. I think this year is going to be a cracking good Christmas, don't you?"

"Whatever you say, dearest," Cam said, too busy trying to calm his still pounding heart to scold her use of cant. "Whatever you say."

Chapter Three

"An unusual text for one's first sermon, don't you think, Amelia? 'Do unto others'?"

"I suppose The Reverend Mr. Stephen Fleming will want us to start knitting socks and hats for the gypsies' Christmas presents next, my dearest Cecily."

The opening notes of the last hymn covered their snickers. Cam rose with the rest of the congregation, determined not to turn around in the St. Cloud family pew and glare at Cecily Tarwater and her sister, Amelia Baker. For more than twenty-five years, they ran the Ladies Auxiliary, the Altar Guild and anything else at All Souls they could pull into their clutches. While a rector might be in charge of the parish's souls, the immovable force of Tarwater, Baker and their crony Grace Hopewell, kept an ironclad grip on every social aspect of All Souls. It was rumored Cecily and Amelia kept their husbands— Hiram and William, the Vestry's Senior and Junior wardens respectively—under their thumbs as well. As did Grace Hopewell, whose husband Wilfred also served on the vestry. Decisions made by these gentlemen and those who served with them, more than suggested a strong influence by their wives.

As he joined his voice with the others, Cam's gaze flickered toward Miss Fleming in the pew opposite his. Her smile suggested *she* was satisfied with her brother's sermon.

It also made her look uncommonly pretty. Health bloomed in her face and her eyes sparkled with an unfeigned joy. Odd he hadn't noticed it in their earlier meetings. Miss Amanda Fleming was no doubt—when she and her dog weren't scaring horses and their riders—a very happy young woman.

As if aware of his scrutiny, she turned her head in his direction. Twin spots of pink covered her cheekbones, but her gaze did not falter. Cam nodded and she turned back to her hymnal.

The singing ended and the congregation headed toward the parish hall. Cam stepped into the aisle where he was met by Mrs. Tarwater and Mrs. Baker. Stifling a sigh, he bowed. "Good morning, ladies. I hope I find you well."

"Very well indeed, my lord." Mrs. Tarwater made a deep curtsey. "What did you think of our new rector's sermon?"

"To the point," Cam said. "I prefer that in a sermon."

"I noticed Lady Perdita in the choir," Mrs. Baker said. "Such a beautiful voice. And so accomplished. She must be looking forward to her come-out next spring."

"She is," Cam agreed. "I understand you ladies have organized a reception in the parish hall to welcome Mr. Fleming and his sister?"

The women exchanged smug smiles. Cam doubted very much if either one actually did any of the work. They excelled in ordering others to do their bidding and then took all the credit.

"It's the least we can do," Mrs. Tarwater said primly.

"After all, the Good Book commands us to practice hospitality," Mrs. Baker added.

"So it does," Cam said, "as well as practicing charity as Mr. Fleming's sermon reminded us. If you ladies will excuse me, I must find Lady Perdita." He bowed and left for the parish hall. A few moments in their company was all he could tolerate.

The parish hall was crowded, probably as much for the refreshments as to welcome Mr. and Miss Fleming. They stood together, greeting their new parishioners. Cam looked over the room for the still absent Perdita, resigned himself to his fate and took his place at the end of the line behind Mrs. Baker and Mrs. Tarwater. Perdita could take twenty minutes just to hang up her choir robe and put away her music.

"But at least seein' as 'ow you're twins, we ain't gonna have no problem in tellin' ye apart even if ye are brother and sister," Squire Henry Beecham, a local yeoman farmer chortled while he pumped Mr. Fleming's hand.

"I certainly hope not," Mr. Fleming's expression of mock horror produced a hearty laugh from the squire.

"Ye might be all right," he said, slapping Mr. Fleming's arm. "Least ways you've got a sense of humor, which is more than old Percy—him that was rector before you—had."

"Really, Squire Beecham," Mrs. Tarwater said with a loud sniff. "One shouldn't speak ill of the dead."

"Ain't no concern of ye what I say to the rector," Beecham said gruffly. "'Specially if 'tis true. Mr. Smythe could put a dead man to sleep with 'is sermonizing. I like the Gospel preached simple and to the point."

"Stephen turned down a teaching position at Balliol College at Oxford to accept the earl's kind offer of the living at All Souls," Miss Fleming said proudly.

"Well, we're mighty glad to have you." Beecham looked back at Mr. Fleming. "Ye should come by the farm and see one or two of my horses if ye think you might be wanting to enter the sleigh race. I've got a Tilbury sleigh I can loan ye, too. I'll send my boy for ye."

" 'scuse me, please." A tiny woman whose bonnet had seen better days, thrust herself forward as Beecham stumped away. Mrs. Tarwater frowned in disapproval at the intrusion, but the new arrival gave no notice. "Hate to break in, but I've got to get back home 'fore Sadie delivers 'er next litter of pups." She thrust a small basket at the surprised Mr. Fleming. "I've brought you the last of my summer jams, Mr. Fleming." Worry widened her eyes. "Ye do like strawberries, don'cha? I used my ma's old recipe."

"Really, Mrs. Nichols." It was Mrs. Baker's turn to scold. "Mr. Fleming doesn't need any jam."

"Oh, but he *loves* strawberry jam!" Miss Fleming exclaimed. She beamed at Mrs. Nichols before glancing at her brother. "*Don't* you, Stephen?"

"Y-yes. It's quite my favorite." Mr. Fleming moved the cloth covering the basket's contents. "How very nice of you, Mrs....?"

"Nichols. Hattie Nichols." The little woman shot Mrs. Baker a triumphant glance and Cam coughed back his laugh. It was well-known in the village that Mrs. Baker—even though her cook helped her—could not master the art of jam-making, no matter how hard she tried.

"But there's more than jam in here," Mr. Fleming said. He reached into the basket and held up a small package neatly wrapped and tied up with string. "What do we have here?"

"It's a present for your sister," Mrs. Nichols said shyly. "Just a little sumpin' I made for her."

"Let me see, Stephen." Miss Fleming took the package and untied the string to hold up two lacy handkerchiefs. "You made these for me?"

"Yes'um. A lady can always use a handkerchief, carn't she?" The worry returned to Mrs. Nichols's face.

"But they're beautiful," Miss Fleming praised. "Look, Stephen. See how tiny the stitches are. They're so fine and delicate I shall have to be very careful not to sneeze too hard in them."

Color flooded Mrs. Nichols' face. "Ah, go along with ye, Miss."

"You must come and have tea with us at the rectory," Miss Fleming said. "And we shall have some of your jam with Mrs. Crawford's wonderful scones."

The woman darted a glance at Mrs. Tarwater and Mrs. Baker and her color deepened, "Ar, I carn't do that, Miss." She glanced towards the doorway, before jerking a curtsey. "I hafta go see after my Sadie."

She bolted from the room without a backward glance and Mrs. Tarwater gave the Flemings a patronizing smile. "You might want to be careful about that jam, Mr. Fleming," she said. "Hattie Nichols has any number of dogs running about her home. It's not the cleanest one in your parish. And as for the handkerchiefs, I've no doubt she bought them from a passing tinker. She's such a simple soul, she probably just wanted to impress you."

"She did." Something resembling anger flared in Miss Fleming's eyes. "I'd say her kindness in bringing us these gifts was a perfect example of Stephen's sermon this morning. Did you arrive in time to hear it? For it was a message you certainly—"

"There you are, Cam." Perdita's voice broke into what was about to become a very lively discussion—too lively for the parish hall. "I'm sorry I'm late, but the choirmaster just asked me to sing a solo on Christmas

Eve and we were going over the music. He wants me to sing *Rejoice* from *Messiah*. Isn't that *marvelous?*"

"Marvelous," Cam echoed trying not to groan out loud at the answering anger that sparkled in Mrs. Tarwater's eyes. The first thing she would do when her husband returned from his trip to London would be to tell him about this conversation with Miss Fleming.

Perdita took Miss Fleming by arm. "Come, Miss Fleming. You must let me introduce you to some of our younger folks. No doubt you've been so busy setting up the rectory that you've not had time to meet them. I'll bring her back soon, Mr. Fleming."

Still talking, she pulled Miss Fleming beside her. Cam had never been more grateful for his beloved sister's propensity to chatter or to not recognize a socially awkward situation even when she walked right into it.

"Well," Mrs. Tarwater said tightly. "I mustn't keep you from getting a cup of tea, Mr. Fleming. Come, Amelia."

She strode away, a wide-eyed Mrs. Baker trailing after her. Still clutching the basket, Mr. Fleming shrugged helplessly at Cam. "Sisters," he said. "What can you do with them?"

"Indeed," Cam said. "Indeed."

Especially yours.

Chapter Four

"Cecily Tarwater, Amelia Baker and Grace Hopewell are just old biddies who can't keep their noses out of everyone else's business—especially the first two. It's no wonder their husbands go to London so often on business." Lady Perdita gave her horse Bandit, a gentle nudge with her foot. "I'd stay away too if I were them."

Much to Amanda's relief, Lady Perdita appeared on horseback at the rectory after luncheon with a mounted groom and a gleaming chestnut mare named Daisy for Amanda. After Stephen's gentle, but firm reprimand after church regarding the way she spoke to the wives of the senior and junior wardens, Amanda felt grateful for the chance to escape for an hour or so. She was still smarting a bit from his horrified reaction when she told him about her and Hamish's encounter with St. Cloud at the inn, after his and Lady Perdita's visit.

"Mandy, please, please be careful," he had begged. "I know you mean well, but please try not let other people annoy you into speaking your mind. Especially the earl."

After riding back to Heart's Ease, the groom was quickly dispatched, and the two young women set forth for an afternoon of riding over the estate.

The day turned colder, and the snow crunched beneath their horses' hooves. A breeze ruffled the ribbons of their riding hats, but the cloudless blue sky, stretched above them like a landscape in a Dutch painting. Amanda laughed at her new friend's delicious description of the three ladies and asked, "Are you always so forthright, Lady Perdita?"

"Oh, please do call me Perdita," the younger woman begged. "Or at least do so when we're alone. People at my school were so afraid of my brother Cam being an earl, I never really felt as though I had any friends. Either the staff feared I'd be unhappy and he would move me to another school, or the other girls only wanted to know about him and not about me."

"They wanted you to play matchmaker," Amanda guessed. "Praise their virtues so he might want to meet them, fall in love and marry them."

"Exactly." Perdita waved her riding crop in the air. "But they were all much too young and far too silly for him. Cam doesn't like silliness. And he especially dislikes it when women are too outspoken."

Women like me, you mean. Amanda absently stroked Daisy's neck. "Stephen often has to caution me about speaking my mind," she admitted. "He says it's not ladylike."

"Aren't brothers sometimes the biggest boors?" Perdita groaned. "Cam always scolds me for the same thing. But sometimes the words just tumble out of me. I simply can't help it."

"How well I know," Amanda agreed. "Has any lady lived up to his lordship's expectations?"

Perdita shrugged. "There's Lucy Guest, Viscount Pembroke's daughter. She's a little older than I am and a *perfect* lady. She never has a hair out of place, always wears that little smile and never says, much less does, anything troublesome. I like her, but she wouldn't know how to say boo to a goose."

Amanda could not stop her laughter. "You do indeed speak your mind, don't you, Perdita?"

Perdita joined in Amanda's mirth. "I suppose I shouldn't, but sometimes it's so much fun to say what one thinks. I'd like to see Lucy's face if I did say something outrageous. Cam has known her for ages and I think he likes her well enough. She just finished three years at a terrifically expensive finishing school in Darbyshire before making her bow this past spring. Lucy loves pretty clothes and she's always bang up to the knocker, so it's a good thing her papa is plump in the pockets or he'd be on the rocks from the cost of her wardrobe. Not that she needs fancy dresses. She's so pretty she could wear a kitchen maid's dress and still be stunning."

She paused for breath, and Amanda tried not to laugh at Perdita's use of popular cant. Before she could start up again, Amanda asked, "With all her advantages,

37

has Miss Guest expressed no interest in anyone? Or received any offers?"

"She could get any proposal just by crooking her little finger," Perdita scoffed. "But she turned down half a dozen requests just to call on her, or so the on-dits say, which is why I think she's waiting for Cam to propose. I think he will ask her to marry him any day now, but he'll have to wait until Lucy's great aunt Adelaide arrives. She's devoted to Lucy and would never give her approval if a proposal were made and she wasn't there. Lucy is certainly suitable enough."

"Suitable?" Amanda pulled Daisy to a stop. "You mean he doesn't love her?"

Perdita shrugged. "You have to understand about Cam's sense of duty," she said. "He's terribly proud of being Saint Cloud. Our family goes back five hundred years and he would die rather than dishonor our name. Not just anyone can become his countess. It's a huge responsibility. He would never marry someone who's not up to the task."

"And you, Lady Perdita?" Amanda affected the haughty tone of a dowager. "Whom shall you marry?"

"I shall marry only for love," Perdita said stoutly. "Of course, it won't hurt a bit if he's young and rich and handsome. A real out-and outer who will agree with me on everything."

"You're a lady," Amanda reminded her. "You can't marry a man who doesn't meet with your brother's approval."

"I'm so tired of being reminded that," Perdita groaned again. "Sometimes I long to do something so outrageously un-ladylike, that all those old village busybodies will have the vapors at the same time."

Amanda laughed again. "What on earth would you do? Become a blue-stocking?"

"Not quite *that* outrageous," Perdita said. "But I'll share a secret with you. I've always longed to ride astride. It seems like it would be such wild fun. Have you ever ridden astride, Amanda?"

"Well—"

"You have?" Perdita stopped Bandit by a large stump and stared at Amanda, excitement brightening her eyes. "Really?"

"Yes," Amanda admitted reluctantly. "On my parents' farm when I was younger. Stephen and I would race, and riding astride made it easier."

"Then let's ride astride right now and have a race. I'll bet Bandit here is just itching for one." Perdita started to dismount.

"Perdita, we can't," Amanda protested. "Our brothers would kill us both. I'm sure the earl won't like it. And besides, we're riding side-saddle."

"Fiddlesticks! What they don't know won't hurt them," Perdita insisted, continuing her ascent. "Come help me with these skirts, Amanda."

"Perdita, I really think we should not—"

"Are you afraid I'll beat you?" Perdita challenged. "We'll just race to that big tree over there and back."

"But it must be at least half a mile," Amanda said. "We can't race astride that far in a side-saddle."

"Why not?"

Oh Lord, what am I getting myself into? Withholding her sigh, Amanda got off her horse, helped Perdita re-mount so she sat astride before getting back on Daisy, and sitting in the same fashion.

"This certainly feels...unusual," Perdita admitted, guiding Bandit in a circle. "Very unusual. I wonder that men like it."

"I still think this a bad idea, Perdita," Amanda cautioned. "If your brother finds out—"

"But he won't," Perdita said. "Not unless you tell him. Are you ready?"

Knowing further protests were useless, Amanda gave in to the inevitable. "Ready."

"One. Two. Three. Go!" Perdita shouted, and they were off.

For someone riding astride for the first time, Perdita was very good. The air rushed by Amanda's ears, and she gripped Daisy with her knees. The mare was smaller and lighter than Bandit, but appeared to have no trouble keeping up. The tree loomed ahead, and a sudden gust of breeze struck them, blowing off Amanda's hat and freeing her loosely piled hair. Her curls tumbled about her shoulders, but she leaned low, and lightly kicked Daisy's ribs.

"Come on, Daisy!" she shouted. "Come on, girl!"

"Oh, this is wonderful!" Perdita shouted as they galloped side by side. "I think from now on, I shall ride astride all the time! What a capital idea!"

Amanda laughed, caught up in the excitement. Then as she looked ahead at the stump, her heart plummeted to her toes. "Oh my goodness," she gasped. "It's your brother."

Sure enough, standing up in the back of a small, open carriage stopped by the stump, his arms folded over his chest, was the Earl of St. Cloud. Even from the remaining distance, Amanda knew he was angry—very angry.

Perdita must have seen her brother as well, because she sat up in the saddle and urged Bandit to a walk.

The earl still didn't move, only stood staring at them. Beside him on the seat sat an extraordinarily beautiful young woman in a bright blue traveling ensemble.

"Who's that?" Amanda whispered as they slowly approached the carriage and its occupants. The woman spoke to the earl, who nodded. The driver sat expressionless behind a lone horse.

"That's Lucy Guest," Perdita whispered back. "The girl I told you that Cam might marry."

"I see." Amanda's fingers curled around Daisy's reins. Lucy Guest was a Dresden miniature come to life, all pink cheeks against porcelain skin and big blue eyes. Blonde curls peeked out from her bonnet, and her composed features completed the image of a perfect lady and the perfect bride for an earl.

Certainly not like a young woman who went riding astride like a hoyden, or worse.

"Hello, Cam," Perdita called as they reached the carriage. "Hello, Lucy. I didn't know you were in Huntingdown."

"We've only just arrived," Lucy Guest said serenely. "I'm delighted to see you again, Perdita." She blinked several times and her expression shifted into one of faint horror. "My goodness, are you riding *astride?*"

Perdita shot Amanda a quick, defiant glance before turning it on Lucy and the earl. "Yes, we are," she said. "Amanda was telling me how she used to race her brother by riding astride, and so I challenged her to a race doing the same. Lucy, this is my friend, Amanda Fleming. Her brother is the new rector at All Souls. Amanda, this is Lucy Guest, Viscount Pembroke's daughter."

"Perdita, what do you think you're doing?" St. Cloud's soft voice bit off the words in a slow, dangerous rhythm and a chill slid down Amanda's spine. A tiger's growl would have been less menacing. So would its eyes.

"Racing, Cam." Perdita's voice wobbled, but her gaze at her brother did not waiver.

"Go home, Perdita," he ordered. "We'll discuss this later."

"But—"

"Now, Perdita. I'll have George here come to the rectory later to collect Daisy."

"No, you won't." Perdita raised her chin. "Daisy is *my* horse and I'm going to let Amanda keep her at the rectory so we can go riding again soon. It's silly to drag poor Daisy back and forth—"

"I said we'll talk about this later, Perdita," St. Cloud repeated. "Please go home."

Making a sound suspiciously like a snort, Perdita urged Bandit forward and St. Cloud turned his attention on Amanda. Anger shimmered in the depths of his cobalt-hued eyes as they raked over her, taking in her missing hat and windblown curls. She shivered beneath her habit, and tightened her grip on Daisy's reins, praying he wouldn't see her hands tremble.

"Miss Fleming," St. Cloud said formally. "I would appreciate it if in the future you would not indulge my sister in her whims. As the elder, you should know better than to let her put herself at risk for grave injury or worse."

"I tried to talk her out of it, my lord," Amanda defended. "Really I did."

"Obviously not hard enough, as you telling her of your own experiences riding astride can attest. Perdita is easily led by suggestion, especially by those she admires, which includes you, even after so short an acquaintance. Good day to you, Miss Fleming. You may keep Daisy at the rectory for now. Take us home, George."

The groom waited until St. Cloud was seated before clucking at the horse and turned the carriage around. Miss Guest had not spoken a single word to Amanda, but the set of her mouth told Amanda all she needed to know about the other young woman's opinion of her. It was not one that suggested a hoped for continuing of their recent acquaintance.

There was nothing left for Amanda to do but retrieve her hat, and go home to tell Stephen of her latest blunder.

Chapter Five

She looked like a Viking princess. All wild blonde hair and flashing eyes astride her horse. All she needed was a sword.

"My lord?" Viscountess Emmaline Pembroke raised her voice.

Cam blinked and looked at his guests. Oakley and Mrs. Shelton, the St. Cloud's cook, were setting down the enormous tea trays on a table between Perdita and the Pembrokes. Perdita nodded her acceptance and the servants departed, closing the door behind them.

"I beg your pardon, Lady Emmaline. I was just pondering that very question," Cam said. *Pull yourself together, man! Most definitely not the thing to fall asleep when you've invited guests to tea.*

"I was saying, might we hope you will hold the annual Winter Ball?" the Viscountess asked. "It's been so many years since the last one. And now that Lady Perdita is old enough to act as your hostess, how shall we persuade you?"

Nodding, Cam crossed his legs and said, "I think you're right, Lady Emmaline. This is the perfect opportunity for Perdita to practice her hostess skills. And now that you have arrived, our circle of friends from

45

London is nearly complete." *How on earth did a clergyman's daughter learn to ride astride?*

Lady Emmaline gave him a fond smile. "Shall it be a fancy dress ball or some other kind of event? Lady Perdita, what are your thoughts?"

"I think a formal ball will be wonderful, but I'm sure we'll do whatever Cam thinks is suitable." From behind the safety of the tea table, Perdita fluttered her eyelashes in a parody of innocence. But the set of her smile—so like their mother's when she was crossed—told Cam Perdita's irritation with him over stopping her wild ride with Miss Fleming yesterday afternoon, remained. Galloping over the estate like a hoyden! Surely Perdita saw the folly in such?

"How's the new rector settling in?" Viscount Pembroke's question thankfully changed the subject. "Where'd you find him, St. Cloud?"

"The Reverend Stephen Fleming came highly recommended by the Master of Balliol at Oxford." Cam passed his empty plate to Perdita. "Fleming took a double first there his last year."

"Very impressive," Pembroke said. "Does he preach well?"

"Yes, he does," Perdita announced before Cam could frame a reply. She filled his plate and passed it back to him. "I liked his first sermon very much. I like his sister too."

"Was she the young lady we met with you yesterday when we came to fetch you?" Lucy asked. "How very pretty she is."

Cam's pulse skipped a beat at Lucy's description of Miss Fleming, and prayed she would not reveal just how they'd found her and Perdita. Pembroke prided himself on his daughter's perfect lady-like behavior and frowned on those women who did not meet his exacting standards. The mere thought of a young unmarried lady riding astride would send him into an apoplectic fit, *especially* if that young lady was in the company of his future son-in-law's sister.

Emmaline Pembroke shared her daughter's fragile beauty, except for the calculating shrewdness in her eyes. Every mother wanted the best match possible for her daughter, and Emmaline was no exception. She would use every device at her command to insure Lucy made the grandest of marriages; one the ton would discuss for years to come.

But she was also careful, and not likely to overplay her hand too soon. Cam could have any woman he wanted for his countess and they both knew it. She might not swoon at the thought of her only daughter riding astride, but would have sternly reprimanded Perdita for such behavior. And she certainly would take Miss Fleming to task for allowing Perdita to do so.

Fortunately, Lucy said no more on yesterday's unfortunate meeting, and Cam's eyes sent her silent thanks. "Perhaps Lucy could help Perdita decide on the theme for the Winter Ball," he said. "I can't have the local ladies angry with me for not giving them enough time to plan what they will wear."

"How very kind of you, my lord!" Lady Emmaline declared. "I am quite sure that between the two of them the Winter Ball will have half of London beating a path to the doors of Heart's Ease. Don't you agree, my dear Pembroke?"

"Our Lucy can turn her hand to anything," Pembroke said, smiling broadly at Cam. "Music, painting, even helping to run a household. She does a lot for Lady Pembroke now, don't you Lucy?"

"Yes, Papa," Lucy said obediently. Her confident tone was that of a young woman groomed from birth to run a nobleman's house upon becoming his wife. A perfect lady down to her bones, and one who would never even consider riding astride.

And certainly not one who by any stretch of the imagination would ever look like a Viking princess.

****

"Yes, Miss?" The dark-haired young man peeked cautiously around the half-open cottage door.

"Good afternoon," Amanda said. "I'm Miss Fleming, from the rectory. Is Mrs. Nichols at home?"

The door moved inward and Amanda heard the murmur of voices. Then the door popped fully open and

Hattie Nichols regarded Amanda with open-mouthed astonishment. "Miss Fleming?"

"Good afternoon, Mrs. Nichols," Amanda said shyly. "I hope my calling without an invitation is not an inconvenience?"

"N-no, not at all." The older woman beckoned Amanda to cross the threshold. A welcoming fire crackled in the grate and the aroma of freshly-baked soda bread made Amanda's stomach rumble. From what she could see, the room was immaculate, giving a lie to Mrs. Tarwater's claim that Mrs. Nichols's home was less than clean.

"This here is my grandson, Arthur." Mrs. Nichols pointed at the young man who had retreated to stand behind a wooden chair in the corner. "Arthur, this is Miss Fleming, the new rector's sister."

"I know," Arthur said sullenly. "I saw her at church last Sunday." His expression hovered between apprehension and defiance, and his posture suggested he could bolt at any time.

"How do you do, Arthur?" Amanda asked gently.

"Just fine, Miss. Ma, I'm going out to go work with Tinker." Arthur gave a quick nod in Amanda's direction and slipped into the back of the cottage.

"What brings you out this way, Miss?" Mrs. Nichols remained by the door. "'Tis a good three miles from the rectory to here. Don't get many visitors out this way, 'less them be wantin' jam or vegetables or such.

49

There weren't nothing wrong with the jam I made you and the Reverend, were there?"

"No, indeed," Amanda assured her. "Rather, it was too good and we've eaten almost all of it. Thank you for bringing it to us."

Mrs. Nicolas's features relaxed. "That's all right then," she said, beckoning Amanda forward. "I was just about to have a bit of tea. Got soda bread and fresh churned butter to go with it, too. Could you stay and have some with me?"

"I'd be delighted," Amanda said. "But first, might I explain the reason for my visit?"

"Yes, ma'am." Mrs. Nicolas folded her hands and waited.

Amanda took the large basket from over her arm and gave it to her hostess. "I was inspecting the church linens and found that two of the altar cloths have somehow become torn. They're rather long rips, and I'm not very good with a needle or else I would do the repairs myself. Those handkerchiefs you brought me were so fine, I hoped you might mend the linens. Stephen will pay you, of course."

"Me? You want me to mend the church's linens?" Mrs. Nichols's mouth fell open again. "Mrs. Hopewell always does the sewing for the church. She's on the Altar Guild, and I'm not. She's the one you want, not me."

"But I've not seen her work," Amanda said. "I'd much rather you mend them, unless you're too busy."

Satisfaction gleamed in Mrs. Nicholas's eyes. "I'd be pleased to make the repairs, Miss," she said, then placed the basket on a small sideboard. "Sit you down on that sofa there, and we'll have tea. Let me have your coat."

When they were seated and Mrs. Nichols had served them, Amanda asked, "How is your dog, Sadie? How many puppies did she have?"

"Six," Mrs. Nichols said proudly. "Them's all doing fine. I'm taking them to First Monday market to sell come January, after they're weaned. Border Collie pups is a good thing, even if them only watch out fer ye, and not herd nothing."

"And all your other dogs? Tell me about them."

There's just Sadie and Tinker—him who sired her pups," Mrs. Nichols said. "Just them two."

"Oh," Amanda said. "I thought—"

She let her words trail away, but Mrs. Nichols's eyes narrowed. "That Cecily Tarwater told ye I've a pack of dogs running around the house, didn't she?" she demanded. "Tried to say my house weren't clean?"

"Yes," Amanda admitted, "she did."

Mrs. Nichols shook her head. "You best watch your step, around Mrs. Tarwater and Mrs. Baker, Miss," she warned. "Mrs. Hopewell too. You don't want to make no enemies out of them. They're as mean and spiteful as a brood of vipers, they are. They don't like me, and if they knowed you'd called on me, they'd not be happy."

"But why don't they like you?"

A grin of delight lit up Mrs. Nichols's features. "'Cause my son beat Mrs. Baker's son in the earl's annual Christmas sleigh race ten years ago," she said. "Put her noise right out of joint 'cause my Billy won the twenty pound prize. T'weren't the money, but everyone thought 'cause 'er son's horse cost so much, it'd win. But my Caesar—that's the horse's name, Miss—left 'em all behind. 'Course now, he's got a touch of the rheumatism, but he can still run like the wind when he has a mind."

"It seems that the ladies of the Altar Guild like to have their own way," Amanda said.

"That's sure as Gospel," Mrs. Nichols agreed with a nod.

"Like I said, you best not be seen too much with me. Don't want no trouble for you or your brother."

"The earl gave Stephen his living, not Mrs. Tarwater, Mrs. Baker or Mrs. Hopewell," Amanda said crisply. "As long as the earl is satisfied, that's all that matters."

"If you say so, Miss." Mrs. Nichols sounded doubtful. "But if they'd spread rumors about my house being dirty, they'd probably find reason to find fault with you."

"I'm not afraid of them," Amanda said. "I shall be friends with whoever I choose. Shall we be friends?"

Satisfaction sparkled in the woman's eyes. "Thank you, Miss. I'd like that."

They chatted for several more minutes about her dogs and Amanda told her about Hamish. Mrs. Nichols shared one or two bits of harmless gossip and Amanda found herself laughing at the descriptions.

"Well, I've taken up enough of your time." Amanda drank her remaining tea and put her cup aside. "Thank you for your hospitality."

"The earl, now, he's a fair man," Mrs. Nichols said unexpectedly. "Couldn't ask for no better, him and his father, and his father before him. Lord Cameron's a bit stiff sometimes, but he's fair and takes good care of Lady Perdita."

"I've noticed that," Amanda said slowly. Under his haughty manner, St. Cloud had a heart—at least where his sister was concerned. "Is there anything else you can tell me about Huntingdown? Something that my brother might need to know?"

"Well," Mrs. Nichols said thoughtfully. "It would be nice to have a school for the tenants' children."

Amanda blinked. "You mean there *isn't* a school?" she asked. "But how do the children learn to read and write?"

Mrs. Nichols shrugged. "They don't, most times. The gentry's got governesses livin' in their houses and when their boys is old enough, they go away to them big fancy schools. But the tenants' children ain't got one of their own. Be nice if they could at least learn to read the

Bible a bit. Most times they go into service or work on the land. Not much call to read and write in those jobs."

"No, I suppose not." Amanda paused and asked, "Do you read, Mrs. Nichols?"

"Yes, Miss, I do," her hostess said proudly. "Enough so's I taught my own children how. Them's got good jobs 'cause of it. Taught Arthur too. He used to help Sexton Reid at All Souls before—"

She stopped, and began to gather up the cups and plates. "I can send some soda bread home for your brother if you think he'd like it, Miss." Anger had tightened her features, but her voice was carefully neutral.

"He'd like it. What happened at All Souls, Mrs. Nichols?" Amanda asked. "Why isn't Arthur helping Sexton Reid anymore?"

"'Cause Mrs. Tarwater and her friends convinced Mr. Smythe that a *tenant's* grandson didn't need to be working at All Souls," Mrs. Nichols said bitterly. "They've got fancy ideas and said it would make the church look bad, though they tried to say—or they got their husbands to say—All Souls couldn't afford to pay 'em both. Arthur weren't paid much, and he did a lot of heavy lifting and polishing for Sexton Reid. Sexton Reid was gonna talk to Mr. Smythe about Arthur training to be verger one day after Verger Hawkins retires, but after the vestry did what they did, Sexton Reid didn't bother. Nearly broke Arthur's heart. He loves All Souls and would do anything for it. It's all I can do to make him come to church with me now. That's why he was unfriendly-like to you."

"I see," Amanda said quietly. It seemed the triumvirate of Tarwater, Baker and Hopewell was more powerful than she thought. She would have to be careful. "Thank you for the tea. Now I have two friends in Huntingdown—you and Lady Perdita."

"I'm proud to name you friend, Miss," Mrs. Nichols said, handing Amanda the napkin-wrapped soda bread.

Outside, as she climbed into the wagon, Amanda said, "Just bring the linens by the church when you're finished."

"I'll do that, Miss," Mrs. Nichols called from the doorway. "Thank you for thinking of me."

Driving home, Amanda mulled over what Mrs. Nichols told her about the Altar Guild. Hopefully, Amanda would find a way to work with them. Already, Stephen loved All Souls, and Amanda would not let her outspokenness cost him his living.

But she would not curtail her new friendship with Mrs. Nichols. A friend was a friend, and Amanda would not let the Altar Guild choose her friends for her. If they proved to be like the ladies at the other churches, she would need all the friends she could get.

But first, she would talk to Stephen about starting a Sunday school for the tenants' children.

Chapter Six

"It's outrageous! Asking Hattie Nichols to mend the altar linens instead of me. That's *my* job on the Altar Guild! It always has been!" Grace Hopewell—who at the moment did not live up to her first name—actually stamped her foot.

"What does it matter who mends the altar linens as long as they are mended?" Cam asked, putting aside Heart's Ease quarterly accounts.

"Hattie Nichols is *not* on the Altar Guild," Mrs. Hopewell fumed, "as if such a thing was possible! She's a *tenant's* widow." Her expression suggested that even saying the word 'tenant' gave her a particular pain. "Who does Miss Fleming think she is?"

"If I recall, Mrs. Nichols once sewed for my mother," Cam said coldly, ignoring her question about Miss Fleming. "Would you suggest that the late Countess of St. Cloud would have a less than superior seamstress sew for her?"

A bright red flooded Mrs. Hopewell's cheeks. "Of course not, my lord, but Miss Fleming had the audacity to ask Hattie without a word to me, or anyone else on the Guild! Since when does the rector's sister have authority over the Altar Guild?"

"I suggest you take this up with Miss Fleming or the rector." Cam picked up the accounts again. "Is there anything else you need from me, Mrs. Hopewell?"

Mrs. Hopewell's mouth tightened. "No, my lord."

"Then I wish you a pleasant afternoon," Cam said. "Oakley will show you out."

Knowing a dismissal when she heard one, Mrs. Hopewell curtsied, muttered her farewell and left, banging the door behind her.

"Women," Cam announced to the room. "Why do they choose to pick battles over such nonsense?" He supposed after he and Lucy married, she would take her place on the Altar Guild. Imagining Lucy directing the haughty Mrs. Tarwater and Mrs. Baker, made him laugh. Lucy would not care who mended the church linens.

But why would Miss Fleming have not mended the linens herself? Surely she had some skills with a needle? Perhaps she was too busy perfecting her horseback riding skills to bother. Images of her stepping from the mist at their first meeting, and then later galloping toward him like a Fury on horseback, flooded his brain.

Damn, why did his heart suddenly bang against his ribs in such an alarming manner? Amanda Fleming, an attractive woman? A beautiful woman? Ridiculous!

A brisk knock sounded from the other side of the door, and grateful for the interruption, Cam pushed the accounts aside again. "Come in," he called.

The door opened and the object of his thoughts burst into the room, clutching a shawl-wrapped bundle to her chest. Oakley followed, his brows knit together. Cam rose at once. "Miss Fleming?"

"It's Hamish," she gasped. "I was coming to invite Perdita to tea this afternoon. A rabbit ran in front of us and he-he-." A sob broke her voice and for a moment she did not speak.

"It would appear, my lord, that Miss Fleming's dog ran in front of one of our wagons. Quinn from the stables was returning from the village with foodstuffs," Oakley interjected. "He has been warned about driving too fast along the road to Heart's Ease. At least he had the presence of mind to bring Miss Fleming here."

"You were walking to Heart's Ease from the rectory?" Cam asked. "But it's two miles from here!" He vaguely recalled being forced by a female friend to read a still rather new novel in which the heroine walked three miles through the country to visit an ailing sister, enchanting the hero with her windblown appearance.

"Stephen is paying calls on a new parishioner who lives in Fairfax," Miss Fleming gulped. "He took the wagon and since it was such a beautiful day I decided to…" her voice faltered again.

"Put Hamish on the desk," Cam ordered. "Let's have a look at him."

Miss Fleming came forward and carefully put her bundle on Cam's desk. She peeled back the shawl and the Scottie cried out in pain, his eyes wide and frightened.

"Well, at least he's alive." Cam blew out a sigh of relief.

"But he's injured!" Miss Fleming cried. "Who takes care of injured animals in these parts? The farrier?"

"The closest farrier is six miles from here," Cam said. "Do you think Hamish would be more comfortable in your arms or in a basket with a blanket?"

Miss Fleming bit her lip. "He'd want me to hold him. Why would he need to be in a basket?"

"Because we're going to take him to Hattie Nichols's cottage," Cam told her. "If there's anyone who knows how to take care of dogs, injured or not, it's her."

He looked past her at Oakley. "Tell Quinn to bring the cart back 'round, would you please, Oakley?"

"He's waiting outside, my lord. I think he knew you'd want him."

"At least he's showing some sense." As gently as he could, Cam wrapped Hamish in the blanket and gave him to Miss Fleming.

He led her from the room and outside to the porch. At the foot of the steps, a tearful Quinn waited beside the cart with its lone horse.

"I'm sorry, Miss," he said, tears choking his voice. "I didn't see your dog, honest I didn't. He just ran right in front of me."

"Hamish can't resist the temptation to chase rabbits," Miss Fleming said as Cam guided her down the steps. Beneath his gloved hand, she trembled. "I'm sure you didn't mean any harm."

Cam saw Quinn give him a fear-filled glance. "I'm sorry, my lord," the young man said.

"Let us be grateful it wasn't a child, Quinn," Cam said sternly after helping Miss Fleming up onto the back seat. "You've been warned about driving too fast, haven't you?"

Quinn lowered his head. "Yes, my lord. I was just thinking 'bout how grand it would be to take part in the holiday race."

"Well, you can practice your skills and get us to Mrs. Hattie Nichols's cottage as quickly and safely as you can. And take the back roads. Do you think you can do that?"

"Yes sir!" Quinn barely waited for Cam to take his place beside Miss Fleming before he sprang onto the driver's seat and shouted, "Get you up, Wellington!"

The horse seemed to catch the urgency in Quinn's voice and took off. Miss Fleming leaned against the seat's high back, cradling Hamish to her chest. Beneath the rumble of the wheels, Cam heard her croon to him, as she stroked the dog's head. A single tear rolled down her cheek and Cam fought a rising urge to shove Quinn aside and take the reins himself. Never had the distance to Hattie Nichols's home seemed so long.

But soon enough they stopped at her cottage. As though she expected them, the little woman stood outside, her eyes bright with curiosity.

"Miss Fleming's dog, Hamish, has been injured, Mrs. Nichols." Cam did not wait for the usual pleasantries. "Can you help him?"

Mrs. Nichols's expression shifted to one of professional concern and she came forward. "I'll do my best. Hand him down to me, Miss," she said, holding out her arms.

Miss Fleming lowered Hamish to her and then, not waiting for Cam to assist her, scrambled down from the cart and followed Mrs. Nichols. Cam did the same.

Inside the cottage, Mrs. Nichols placed Hamish on a large table in the corner and gently pulled back the shawl.

"So you had a bit of an accident, did you?" she crooned, stroking the Scottie's ears. "Were you dreaming of chasing a stag across the wilds of the moors or just having a bit of a run?"

Hamish's tail thumped feebly in response, but when she lightly ran her hands over his side, he whimpered, and tears pooled in Miss Fleming's eyes. " Will he be all right?" she asked.

Mrs. Nichols's hands continued their exam and then with surprising speed and skill, gently turned the dog over on his other side. Hamish yelped but Mrs. Nichols began to sing a low, soft tune and he quieted. After a minute, she straightened and smiled at them.

"There's nothing broken, Miss," she said. "And his heartbeat is strong. Run in front of a horse, did he?"

"How did you know that?"

Mrs. Nichols grinned. "I've had a Scottie or two in my time. If something is moving, they're going to chase it. What Hamish needs is rest and as little movement as possible. That's asking a lot for a Scottie, but he's going to be fine. I've a syrup with essence of poppy in it that I can mix up for you. If you put it in some milk, it will help him stay still. Let me get it for you."

She hurried from the room, and to Cam's horror, Miss Fleming burst into tears.

"Oh, Hamish," she sobbed. "I'm so sorry."

"It's not your fault," Cam said, his brain scrambling to remember everything his father taught him to do when women cried. He started by a cautious pat on her shoulder with just his fingertips.

"He could have been killed," she choked out, still crying. "What would I tell Stephen? He adores Hamish! He practices his sermons on Hamish and lets him sleep on the foot of his bed."

"But he's going to be fine," Cam assured her. "You heard what Mrs. Nichols said. Scotties like to chase things, as I can certainly attest."

A laugh broke through her sobs and she turned to him. Tears still streamed down her face, but she gave him a wobbly smile.

"They do, don't they?" She gulped. "Did your ankle ever heal?"

"I think I'll manage," Cam said. Lord, but she was a beauty. Why wasn't she married? "I've even lost the limp."

"Good," she said. "It would be a shame if the Earl of St. Cloud couldn't dance at his own Winter Ball."

She started to dry her cheeks with the back of her hand, and Cam pulled a handkerchief from his greatcoat's pocket, fully intending to offer it to her.

And then a madness seized him. Slowly, carefully, he blotted her tears, moving the cloth over her impressive cheekbones, up to the corners of her eyes. Miss Fleming stood quite still, her gaze riveted on his face, while a warmth spread through Cam's chest as he breathed in a floral essence that called up springtime.

"It would be remiss indeed," he said softly, his handkerchief continuing its work, "if I couldn't dance at the Winter Ball. Perdita would never forgive me if did not open it with her."

"One should never annoy one's sister," Miss Fleming whispered. "We can create quite a fuss if we choose."

"How well I know," he answered, halting his hand, and letting it rest on her cheek. "Brothers live in terror of it."

"As well you should," she said, placing her hand over his. Golden lights shimmered in her eyes, pulling him into their jade depths. "Never underestimate a sister—or a woman for that matter." Her lips beckoned him.

"I'll try to remember that." Cam leaned forward until his mouth hovered over hers and—

"Got it in a nice tight bottle with a dropper," Mrs. Nichols's voice called, and they sprung apart. *Good God, what was he thinking? Kissing the rector's sister?* Cam turned away, shoving his handkerchief back in his pocket, but not before he noted the blush that covered Miss Fleming's face.

"If you'll give him a dropper full in some warm milk during the day, he'll rest just fine," Mrs. Nichols instructed as she joined them. "Two droppers full at night and he'll sleep right through. I've put some on a treat to give him right now."

She produced a tiny biscuit from her apron pocket and gave it to Hamish, who gobbled it up, thumping his tail again.

"I think he must be feeling better," Miss Fleming said, keeping her eyes on her pet. "Hamish never says no to treats."

She looked at Mrs. Nichols with tear-bright eyes. "Thank you so much, Mrs. Nichols," she said, her voice husky. "I'll never be able to repay you for this."

Mrs. Nichols gave her a gentle smile. "He's just badly bruised, that's all, Miss. But I'm glad to help. Maybe this will help Hamish learn not to be so ready to give chase."

"Perhaps it would be best if Miss Fleming took him home now," Cam suggested. It would not do for him to be alone for much longer with Miss Fleming. Her mouth offered too may temptations. He should be grateful he'd insisted on Quinn bringing them instead of doing the driving himself.

Only after Miss Fleming and Hamish were delivered to the rectory, and Cam safely ensconced in his study, did realization strike him hard and swift. What a lucky escape. He must be very careful not to be in Miss Fleming's company again without a roomful of people— preferably several hundred, such as his own wedding reception.

Otherwise, who knew what would happen next?

Chapter Seven

"It won't do, Mr. Fleming, it won't do at all. I'll not have my Grace upset by the likes of Hattie Nichols, or your sister neither." The man's angry voice carried out from Stephen's study and into the parlor.

Not again. The knitting needles stilled in Amanda's hands and she turned her head to wait for her brother's reply. From his basket in the corner, Hamish snored in blissful slumber.

"I'm sure Amanda meant no harm, Mr. Hopewell." Recognizing Stephen's clipped tone, Amanda's heart quickened. Not many things annoyed or angered her twin, but someone questioning her character was on the top of his list of Thou Shalt Not's. "She's a generous soul and would never hurt anyone."

"You'd best be sure she doesn't hurt my Grace's feelings again," Mr. Hopewell insisted. "All Souls isn't the only church around these parts. I can take my tithes someplace else."

"You are free to worship God wherever you choose," Stephen said. "And of course take your tithes with you."

A door slamming, then angry booted feet making their way from the study to the rectory's front door was followed by a second door's slam. It echoed through the house and Amanda put down her knitting. She'd dropped a stitch anyway.

She went to Stephen's study and tapped on the door. Inside, she found him at his desk, elbows propped on its surface, his head in his hands. "Stephen?" she called anxiously. "Have I done much damage?"

He raised his head and smiled. "No, you have not. Saint Cloud told me yesterday about you asking Mrs. Nichols to repair the altar linens when I went to thank him for helping with Hamish. Mrs. Hopewell had already complained to him, but I gather his suggestion to her to talk to one of us didn't take root. I'd have told her the same thing. Silly business, making such a fuss about repairing the altar linens. But Mandy—"

Amanda swallowed. "But?"

"Try not to anger the Altar Guild," he urged. "They've helped run All Souls for years. I know the triumvirate of Tarwater, Baker and Hopewell seem an immovable force, but for my sake, try to be nice to them. Please?"

"How did you guess I call them, 'the triumvirate'?" Amanda asked. "And don't tell me it's because we're twins and we think alike."

His familiar grin replaced his worried expression. "It's the only reason I can fathom for it. It wouldn't do to suggest to our neighbors that we're mind readers."

"No indeed," Amanda agreed. "What about Mr. Hopewell?"

"If he wants to leave and take his tithes with him, then he's welcome to do so," Stephen said firmly. "I've had a look at the church's accounting books, and Mr. Hopewell needs to be reminded that tithes are supposed to be ten percent of one's income. He's one of the wealthiest men in the area, but you'd never know it from the amount he's given to All Souls over the years. I think if that piece of news got out, his days on the Vestry might be numbered."

His grin turned wicked and Amanda could not stop her laughter. "I know that grin," she accused. "You're plotting something, aren't you?"

"I've been struggling with the topic for this week's sermon. It's the first Sunday in Advent, so I want to be especially memorable." A satisfied gleam entered Stephen's eyes. "I think I'll talk about the widow's mite along with a gentle reminder that sometimes it's not how much you give, but the intent and spirit with which you give it. Yes, that will do quite nicely, but it will probably be wasted on Mr. Hopewell."

"Oh, Stephen," Amanda said through her laughter. "I do love you."

"That's good, since I'm your only brother." He picked up the quill and pointed it at her, assuming an expression of mock sternness. "I love you too, but think about a way to get on the triumvirate's good side. Ask for their help with something and try to sound sincere when you do."

"Yes sir." Amanda gave him a smart salute. "Have you given any more thought about starting a Sunday school for the tentants' children?"

"Yes, but I want to wait until after Christmas," Stephen said, dipping his quill into the inkpot. "You can begin planning the lessons if you like. But write those invitations first and send them out before you go to bed tonight. Oh, and one more thing. I've had a letter from my friend George Winterson. He's accepted a living in Hampshire after the holidays, but being a bachelor with no family, has no place to go for Christmas."

"Invite him here," Amanda said. "We have plenty of room."

"There we go with our mind-reading again," Stephen said. "And it's a good thing I knew you would say that, because I've already invited him. Now, go write to the triumvirate."

Laughing, Amanda left him to his sermon and returned to her knitting. She tried to concentrate on her stitches and force the conversation between Stephen and Mr. Hopewell into the back of her mind, only to have it replaced by her persistent thoughts about Cameron Hunt—thoughts that try as she might to banish, would not leave her. Cameron riding beside her as Quinn drove them to Mrs. Nichols's home. Cameron standing with her as they watched Mrs. Nichols examine Hamish. Cameron drying her tears and nearly kissing—

"The Earl of St. Cloud and Lady Perdita Hunt," Alice announced from the parlor doorway.

Amanda rose, dropped the knitting into a nearby basket, and curtsied, grateful her trembling knees didn't give way and send her to the floor. "Good afternoon, my lord, Lady Perdita."

Merciful heavens, it should be a sin for a man to be so handsome. In his coat of dark green superfine, buff breeches, perfectly tied neck-cloth, and gleaming boots, the Earl of St. Cloud would have given Beau Brummell a run for his money. Amanda's throat tightened as she imagined him in wedding finery while he stood waiting at the altar for Lucy. He would be too splendid for words.

"Good afternoon, Miss Fleming," St. Cloud said, executing a perfect bow. "I hope our calling without an invitation is not inconvenient, but we wanted to see how Hamish was progressing."

"He is well, thank you," Amanda said. "Alice, would you bring us some tea please?"

"Yes, Miss Fleming," Alice said cheerfully. "Mrs. Crawford must be a mind reader, 'cause she just took his lordship's favorite Dundee cake out of the oven."

She left, leaving the door open and Amanda gestured at the sofa. "Won't you sit down while we wait?"

"Where is Hamish?" Perdita asked, her face grave with concern. "Did he sleep through the night? Did Mrs. Nichols's poppy syrup help?"

Amanda pointed to the corner. As if on cue, Hamish's snores stopped and he exited from his basket. His steps were unsteady, but upon seeing Perdita, he staggered forward to sit at her feet and give her a mournful look.

"Poor Hamish," she cooed, gently scooping him up in her arms. "Mean, awful rabbit to tempt my Hamish into chasing him. Must tell St. Cloud to get rid of all rabbits!"

Amanda started to laugh but St. Cloud's expression of profound tenderness as he watched Perdita stopped her. He obviously loved his little sister very much.

His gaze flickered in Amanda's direction and a smile slowly spread over his face, knocking the breath from her lungs. She had never seen him smile before.

Sinfully handsome indeed.

"Shall we go see Papa?" Perdita asked Hamish. "Would you like that?"

Hamish's eyes rolled in contentment and he snuggled against Perdita as if to say, "See? This is how a Scottie should be treated."

71

"Is your brother at home, Amanda?" Perdita asked. "I have a question I want to ask him."

"He's in his study, preparing this week's sermon," Amanda said. "But I'm sure he's just waiting for a chance to have tea."

"Then Hamish and I shall go tell him we're here," Perdita said.
She left, still talking nonsense to Hamish, leaving Amanda and Cam alone. Her pulse began a little skipping dance but she managed a smile and asked again, "Won't you be seated, my lord?"

"First, there's this." Coming forward, he pulled a cream envelope from inside his jacket's inner pocket and gave it to her. A large neat hand had addressed it to her and Stephen.

"It's your invitation to the Winter Ball," St. Cloud said. "Perdita and I have almost finished delivering them."

"Do you always deliver them yourselves?"

"Yes, my late mother insisted on it. But we've not held the Winter Ball since she died five years ago."

"You had no hostess?" Amanda guessed. "Is that why?"

He gave her a rueful smile. "Yes. Neither of my parents had any living sisters and the only other female relative, an elderly cousin on my father's side, would have insisted the men wear powdered wigs and have the women dress in farthingales. Not my idea of a good time."

"I should think not," Amanda said, gesturing toward the sofa. When they were seated, she opened the envelope and drew out the embossed card covered in elegant script. "December fifteen," she noted. "The Friday before the third Sunday in Advent and a week before Christmas Eve. Is this another tradition?"

"Yes," he said. "So many people want to spend Christmas in London, my parents always thought it wise to hold the ball the week before, allowing for plenty of time to travel. One never knows about the snow in Surrey." He cleared his throat and fixed his gaze at some point over Amanda's head. "Miss Fleming, my forward conduct toward you yesterday at Mrs. Nichols's home was more than inexcusable and I do beg your forgiveness."

"It's quite all right," Amanda said hurriedly. "You were only trying to calm me in my distress over Hamish. No harm was done and the most important thing is that Hamish is going to recover. Perhaps it would be best not to speak of it again." She stared down at the invitation, trying to think of a safe subject. "Tell me about the Winter Ball."

"The Winter Ball is the most awaited local event of the holiday season here in Huntingdown," Perdita said, coming back into the room, still holding Hamish, with

Stephen right behind her. They settled on the opposite loveseat with Hamish nestled between them.

"Do you have a Little Season here?" Stephen asked.

"Not exactly, but we have lots of parties for the small society that come from London for the holidays," Perdita said. "Cam is letting me plan the Winter Ball, even though I've never done it before. He asked Lucy Guest to help me, but she said the other day she thought I should to it all myself, so that's what I'm going to do."

"I'm sure you'll do it beautifully," Amanda said as Alice entered with the tea tray and left it in her care. After they were all served, St. Cloud said, "What did you want to ask Mr. Fleming, Perdita?"

"I wanted to ask him if we can have lily of the valley on the altar for Christmas Eve," Perdita said, giving Hamish a bite of her cake. "We did when Mama was alive. I always wanted to ask Mr. Tomlinson and Mr. Smythe when they were rectors but Mr. Tomlinson was so stern and Mr. Smythe so silly, I could never bring myself to ask them."

"I told her lily of the valley would be a most appropriate flower to celebrate Christmas," Stephen said. "I'm sure the Altar Guild won't mind either."

Only because she's the earl's sister. "I agree," Amanda said. "Do you have it at the greenhouse at Heart's Ease?"

"Yes," Perdita said. "Our head gardener, Mr. Foust, always keeps pots of it growing for me because he knows how I love it. I think this is going to be a splendid Christmas, don't you?"

"Yes," Amanda agreed, praying it would be so. "Why don't you stay and help me put the final touches on the church decorations I have planned for this Sunday?"

"I would love that!" Perdita clasped her hands together. "May I, Cam?"

"I'll send Quinn round later to fetch you," St. Cloud said. "But not too late, Perdita."

"There's no need to bother your staff, my lord," Stephen said. "Amanda and I can drive Lady Perdita home."

"Thank you." St. Cloud said. "May I ask about the decorations, Miss Fleming?"

"You may not," Amanda said. "It's a surprise."

Chapter Eight

That's the surprise? Cam stared as old Josiah Hawkins, All Souls' venerable verger, raised the torch and lit a purple candle in the evergreen-covered wreath that hung from the church ceiling. Candlelight flickered from miniature wreaths placed on all the windowsills, filling the church with additional warmth. Behind him came a wave of soft gasps and murmurs.

An Advent wreath. So that's what Perdita and Miss Fleming were doing yesterday after tea. Cam stared at his sister in the choir at the front of the church, but she was too caught up in her singing to notice. And it was hard to discern whether her pleasure was in the music only or her part in the decorations.

An Advent wreath. For as long as Cam could remember, All Souls had hovered somewhere between "low" church with very little ceremony, and a middle ground with enough ritual to keep others happy. Incense was never used and he vaguely recalled some fuss long ago about the choir wearing robes as being too "high" church. Ritual mattered little to Cam. A man's relationship with God-with ritual or without it-was his own business.

And from some of the stern expressions and rapid whispers around him, it appeared that some members of the congregation—including Hiram Baker and Samuel Tarwater—felt a new heresy had been thrust upon them. But many of the others smiled and nodded in obvious pleasure, especially the younger members.

He turned his head and found Miss Fleming watching him. She gave him a brief nod, obviously aware of the displeasure swirling around them. Did she not even care what her brother's congregation thought? Cam withheld his sigh and prepared himself for the service to come.

Later during the sermon, Tarwater and Baker's displeasure was stamped on their faces. The Reverend Stephen Fleming in precise but eloquent language, urged his congregation to remember—especially at this time of year—the lesson of the widow's mite and her unhesitating and generous giving. The man must be as naïve in choosing his sermon topics as Perdita was at recognizing snobbery, for his expression radiated nothing but joy as he preached.

At the social hour after church, Hiram Baker lost no time in cornering Cam. "A word with you, my lord?"

"Yes?" Cam's grip on his teacup tightened.

"I'm not of the mind to hear sermons preached about how much I give or don't give to the church!" Anger tightened Baker's features, turning his mouth into a thin line. "I do my bit for All Souls, and I don't come to church to be told otherwise! And since when does All Souls have such trappings? An Advent wreath? What's next, stained glass in our windows?"

The greatest cathedrals in Europe have stained glass windows, Mr. Baker," Cam said calmly. "Chartres Cathedral is a fine example of such. So is Notre Dame in Paris."

"I'd expect that fussiness from the French," Baker said stiffly. "I can't control what they do, anyway. But that Advent wreath, that's something else. Mister Smythe didn't go in for such things. And we got along with him just fine."

"Why didn't you like the Advent wreath, Mr. Baker?" Miss Fleming's voice broke into their conversation. Her gloved hand curled around her prayer book, and the set of her mouth suggested she was preparing for battle with the Senior Warden.

"It's too fussy," Baker argued. "We've never done such things at All Souls."

"Where's the harm?" Miss Fleming asked. "It's a very old, Christian custom. Both of Stephen's last churches had Advent wreaths at Christmas. I suppose that next you'll say you won't support the Sunday school for the tenants' children we hope to start so they can learn to read and write."

"Sunday school for the tenants' children?" Horror widened Baker's eyes to an alarming size. "So they can learn to read and write?"

"Why, yes." Miss Fleming's tone was a degree short of an outright challenge. "Don't you think it's a good idea that all children should be able to read the Gospel?"

"It's your brother's job to preach it to them," Baker insisted. "They don't need to read it, or anything else. Reading will give them ideas above their station and it's sinful for them to try and move out of it."

"Is it really?" Miss Fleming bristled. "Perhaps you should ask my brother exactly where in the Bible it says that before we precede, since he is in agreement of starting the school."

"My lord St. Cloud? What say you?" Baker's tone suggested that man-to-man, they could put a stop to this nonsense.

"Yes, my lord. What say you?" Miss Fleming's gaze at Cam wavered between hope and defiance.

Why can't you be like all the other young ladies of my acquaintance, conventional and even-tempered, instead of stirring up a commotion every other minute? From the first moment I saw you coming out of the mists, I've hardly known a moment's peace.

And I can't get you out of my mind.

"My lord." A red-faced Samuel Tarwater joined them. "Since when do ladies who are not on the Altar Guild provide the after-service refreshments?"

Cam glanced at the long table loaded with a variety of food before looking back at Tarwater. "I don't understand. Is there a problem with the refreshments?"

"My wife and Mrs. Baker always provide them," Tarwater snapped. "It's the responsibility of the Altar Guild, no one else's. It's been that way for years. Why are those other women doing it?"

"*I* asked Mrs. Tidwell and Miss Sylvester to prepare some repast for after the service," Miss Fleming put in.

"You did?" Tarwater's eyes narrowed.

"Yes," Miss Fleming said crisply. "Your wife, Mrs. Baker and Mrs. Hopewell all sent notes 'round to the rectory late yesterday afternoon, saying they were unwell and would be unable to attend services this morning. Please tell them that Stephen can call on them this afternoon if they wish and provide whatever spiritual comfort they might need. But we had to have some kind of refreshment, so I asked Mrs. Tidwell and Miss Sylvester as well as Mrs. Crawford from the rectory to help."

Tarwater's frown deepened. "You should have asked my wife who she would have preferred to prepare the food. My wife's biscuits—"

"—are as hard as rocks." Squire Beecham's booming voice declared as he joined them. "You could break your tooth on 'em if you didn't have a cup of coffee or tea to dunk them in. Them cheese scones today and them little cakes are what I call a real treat. It's 'bout time we had a change from the same old thing. And that Advent wreath was a fine thing. Whose idea was that?"

"Cam, there you are!" Perdita scurried up, with a slightly breathless Lucy Pembroke in tow and Miss Fleming stepped back. An entirely different light entered her eyes and her expression settled into one of grave attention.

Perdita placed her hand on his arm. "Cam, wasn't the Advent wreath just beautiful? Didn't you think so, Mr. Baker? Mr. Tarwater? Amanda let me do most of the work. Did she tell you about the school for the tenants' children she and Stephen—Mister Fleming, that is—are going to start after Christmas? They said I could help, if I wanted. Doesn't that sound like a bang- up good idea?"

"B-bang-up good idea?" Tarwater sputtered while the color drained from Baker's face. Cam had never seen men faint before, but watching the men's expressions at Perdita's use of a beau's cant might provide him with just such a spectacle. Choking back his laugh, he said, "I think the school is a marvelous idea, Perdita."

"Oh, good!" Perdita clapped her hands. "I think this is going to be a cracking good Christmas season, the best one ever! An Advent wreath, a new Sunday school and a special midnight service on Christmas Eve. Doesn't that sound lovely, Squire Beecham?"

"If it means I can hear your sweet voice sing, I'll stay up all night," Beecham praised. A broad grin crossed his face and he winked at other men. "What do you gents think? Don't it sound like a happy Christmas season to you?"

The men muttered what might be any kind of answer before bowing and exiting the parish hall. From the corner of his eye, Cam watched Miss Fleming's mouth tighten in an attempt to hold back her silent laughter. Fearing his own mirth might escape him, Cam looked back at Perdita, whose pretty features were knotted into a mask of confusion.

"Did I say something wrong, Cam?" she asked.

"Not at all, dearest," he said, making sure to avoid Miss Fleming's twinkling eyes. "Not at all."

"Oh, good." Perdita's smile returned. "Lucy says her papa arrived home late last night, and he wants us to come to dinner. May we go?"

"We're expecting several other guests from town to join us late this afternoon," Lucy added. She looked rather stunning in her white coat and matching hat. "Do say you'll come, Cameron. Papa wants our advice on a horse he saw at Tattersal's."

"Of course," Cam agreed. "We'd be delighted to join you. Is your Aunt Adelaide among your guests?" If she were, perhaps tonight would offer the occasion to sound out the old lady about asking for Lucy's hand in marriage.

"No, not yet," Lucy said serenely. "Come let us find Mama and tell her you have accepted. But then of course, we really didn't expect you to refuse."

She paused and looked at the still silent Miss Fleming. "Your Advent wreath was most interesting, Miss Fleming. I'm sure

Papa will come by tomorrow to see what he thinks of it."

The light of challenge returned to Miss Fleming's eyes, but she only inclined her head. For once, she mercifully kept her opinions to herself.

"Ah, there's Mama waving at us." Lucy put her hand on Cam's arm. "She was saying only this morning that Mrs. Owens, our cook, has one or two ideas she wants to share with yours about the menu for the Winter Ball, especially since it's Perdita's first time being its hostess. Shall we go see what Mrs. Owens has in mind?"

And without waiting for his reply, Cam found himself led across the parish hall with Perdita at his side, leaving Miss Fleming behind.

****

"The black or the dark blue, my lord?"

Cam stopped preparing his shaving soap to stare at Higgens's reflection in the large wall mirror as he held up Cam's two sets of evening clothes. "The dark blue," he said.

"Very good, my lord." Higgens said. "Anything special about your cravat for tonight?"

"It's just dinner with the Pembrokes, Higgens," Cam told him as he applied the soap to his face. "Nothing I've not done many times before."

"I only ventured to ask, my lord, because when I went into Huntingdown yesterday to pick up your boots, I heard that the Marquess of Graham as well as Viscount Osborne are to be among the expected dinner guests, and that they are bringing the new horses they purchased for the race."

"Really?" Cam considered this bit of news. Victor Graham and Thomas Osborne always came to Huntingdown to take part in the race. Both were excellent whips, and could boast of several past triumphs, but they had yet to beat any St. Cloud in Huntingdown. The thought nearly made him smile.

But along with their titles, both Graham and Osborne had the money, manners and good looks to make them attractive prospects for any matchmaking mama.

Was the appearance of Graham and Osborne a not-so-subtle warning to Cam that he wasn't the only fish in the sea when it came to Pembroke's only daughter? Did Lady Pembroke think a little healthy competition for Lucy's hand might speed up Cam's proposal, even without the presence of Aunt Adelaide? Cam slid the razor down one side of his face. "Is there anyone else of equal importance among the guests?"

"Not that I have heard, my lord." Higgens stepped back into the closet and Cam continued his shave. It was one thing to have Higgens help him dress for important occasions or trim his hair, but he refused to let another man shave him. Such things were best left for the Regent. Cam studied his face in the mirror and reflected on Higgens's news.

The arrival of Osborne and Graham put a new spin on his matrimonial—or lack of—situation. But did they know about Lucy's great Aunt Adelaide? He would have to watch their attentions to Lucy tonight. Lucy's dainty flattery and past regard for him certainly would have him think they offered no serious threat.

And it wasn't as if he didn't enjoy Lucy's company. She was pretty, accomplished and always conducted herself like the perfect lady that he knew her to be. Not like—

"I beg your pardon, my lord." Oakley spoke from the doorway. "I'm sorry to interrupt you, but there's a problem."

Catching Oakley's tight expression in the mirror, Cam put his razor down on the vanity top. "What is it, Oakley?"

"Mr. Fleming is in your study, my lord," Oakley said. "He asks you to join him at once."

Cam checked his sigh of impatience. Did Miss Fleming not ever talk to her brother? "Tell him I have another engagement. I'll call on him tomorrow."

Oakley cleared his throat. "It seems his sister, Miss Fleming has gone missing, my lord."

"Missing?" Cam gripped the edge of the vanity. "Since when?"

85

"This afternoon, sir. She went riding shortly after three o'clock and hasn't returned. And my lord. . ."

Tension began to coil at the base of Cam's spine. "Yes?"

"Mr. Fleming says that both he and Miss Fleming have a great deal of trouble seeing in the dark," Oakley said solemnly. "Indeed, it quite incapacitates them, so he had Thomas drive him over here. Mr. Fleming is worried that—"

"I understand." Cam wiped the remaining soap from his face. "Tell Mr. Fleming I'll join him shortly, and then ask Quinn to ready Socrates. Ask Mr. Arwine to join me."

"Yes sir." With a nod, Oakley left, concern speeding his usual steady tread down the corridor. Higgens stepped out of the closet and waited.

"Higgens, get out my oldest riding clothes, please." Cam peeled off his dressing gown and tossed it aside.

"But, my lord!" Higgens protested. "What about dining with the Pembrokes?"

"It's only half past six o'clock," Cam said. "I'll instruct George to take Lady Perdita to the Pembrokes if I've not returned in an hour. There's no reason to arrive before eight. We won't dine until nine, so there should be plenty of time."

Worry drew Higgens's eyebrows together. "Do you suppose Miss Fleming has met with some kind of accident, my lord?"

"I have no idea." Cam managed to get out the words through gritted teeth. "Let us pray not."

Because if she hasn't, and this spoils my chance to observe Osborne and Graham with Lucy, I just might wring Miss Amanda Fleming's pretty little neck.

Chapter Nine

Mandy, didn't I ask you to try to get along with the ladies of the Altar Guild? And don't tell me that I didn't mention their husbands. Amanda fought the urge to dismount Daisy and ride her astride at a good hard gallop to dispel her self-annoyance, but settled for a canter. If the triumvirate caught her riding astride, they'd probably demand she and Stephen pack up and leave by next Sunday, but at this moment she really did not care. Such a fuss about the Advent wreath and who prepared the after-service refreshments! It was ridiculous. At Saint Bartholomew's, even with all her problems there, there had never been a to-do about a wreath!

But there had been other battles, and at Good Shepherd as well. Recalling them, Amanda's frustrated mood became one of gloom. The graying afternoon sky matched her mood, and a breeze cut through her white cloak, ruffling the thick ribbon wrapped around her matching hat. She shivered under the mounting breeze's bite and considered turning back. It would be dark soon.

But not just yet. Having Stephen gently scold her—again—during lunch only made her feel worse.

"If there are any complaints from the congregation, then tell them to talk to me," he urged just before he left to see Squire Beecham about a horse and sleigh for the upcoming race. "I'm a bit more diplomatic than you are, Mandy. Please, please let me handle it."

"Diplomatic, my left foot," Amanda muttered as they traveled into a grove of trees. The huge gnarled limbs wove a canopy overhead and she tried to imagine what it would look like in the summer when leaves covered the branches. Would they shut out the light, making the grove a dark and fearful place, hiding every possible danger? Could robbers be hiding here? Wolves? Ghosts?

"I need to stop reading Gothic fiction," she told Daisy, pulling her to a walk by a stream. "I'll have Beowulf creeping out of his cave to drag me away if I keep thinking like this."

Daisy whinnied a soft answer before lowering her head to drink from the stream. Amanda slid off and spying a large boulder, went to sit before it to think.

At least Stephen would be pleased when she told him that she had invited the triumvirate to tea as he asked and they all accepted. She would have to discuss tomorrow's menu with Mrs. Crawford after dinner.

"I'll ask them about All Souls particular Christmas traditions," she yawned. "How they decorate the church on Christmas Eve, about baskets for the local poor, and the like. I'll use Mama's best tea service and silver. Surely, asking for their help should appease them. Then perhaps—" her eyes grew heavy and she tried to keep them open as she yawned again— "their husbands won't stay so cross at me. . ."

Her eyes fluttered open with a start to utter darkness and no horse. Good heavens, how long had she slept? Scrambling to her feet, she called, "Daisy? Daisy, where are you?" Her eyes tried to pierce the gloom but it was too dark. How long had she slept?

And how was she going to get back to the rectory? She was several miles away and didn't have a clue how to find her way home. Above her, the wind whistled through the naked branches and she shivered. Not from the cold, not from the distance to travel, but from the dark.

She was slightly afraid of the dark.

"Breathe slowly and deeply," she coached herself, trying to ignore the thumping of her heart against her ribs. "There's no reason to be afraid. Daisy? Are you there?"

She waited, listening for hooves or a whinny, but only the stream's quiet gurgle answered.

"Think, Amanda," she scolded. "You didn't ride that far into the grove, and here—"she moved her foot to explore the ground—"is surely the path that led you inside. So just slowly walk forward until you are outside, and then across the meadow. Stephen is sure to send someone to search for you."

Knees shaking, she managed to cautiously move forward, hands outstretched. She couldn't remember needing to duck under any low branches, so she shouldn't have to worry about hitting her head. Something crunched beneath her feet and then the texture changed to something soft and whispery. She must be out of the grove and back in the snow-covered meadow. Overhead, a million stars cast their pinpoints of light across the onyx landscape and she tried to recall anything she'd read about navigating by starlight. Wasn't that what sailors did? Surely she could reason it out.

But it was so terribly cold and her trembling increased.

Why in the world hadn't she turned back while it was still light? Stephen would be out of his mind with worry. What would she tell Perdita if something happened to Daisy?

And heaven spare them, what was Amanda going to tell St. Cloud about his horse? She clutched her cloak more tightly about her, and forced that particular idea from her thoughts. If St. Cloud had ever been annoyed with her before now, then this would surely seal her fate.

She stopped and listened. Tandem hooves beating against the ground signaled someone coming, and then a glimmer of light bouncing against the darkness showed that someone carried a lantern. She snatched off her hat and waved it.

"Hello?" she shouted. "Hello, I'm here! Over here!"

The hooves' pounding became a roar and the lantern's gleam grew brighter until even Amanda's eyes could see two fuzzy images on horseback emerge out of the gloom. One surged forward until it was almost on top of her. Amanda stumbled back and then cried out as the horse slowed just enough for a pair of arms to snatch her up onto the saddle, placing her in front of the rider. Sitting so close to him, she could not miss the remarkable features of Cameron Hunt. His scent, faintly sweet with spice notes, enveloped her and she clutched at the lapels of his greatcoat.

"Miss Fleming," he said softly, bringing Socrates to a stop. "Are you all right?"

"Yes," she gasped. "I think so."

His eyes—the expression so like the one the day they met—glittered with a catlike intensity. "Where have you been all this time? Your brother said you left at half past three."

Unsure if the heat scalding her face was from his scrutiny or her own foolishness, Amanda said, "I fell asleep. By a rock near a stream."

"And Daisy? Where is she?"

Tears pricked her eyes but Amanda kept her voice level. "When I woke up, Daisy was gone. I'm sorry. Hasn't anyone seen her?"

"Not when I left."

"Oh, dear," Amanda said miserably. "I'm sorry."

He lifted her chin with his gloved fingers. "You're a great deal of trouble, Miss Fleming, do you know that?"

"I've heard it said so," she admitted, waiting for her heart to stop its furious pace. "I'm sorry. I don't mean to be."

The other rider joined them, lantern in hand. "Got her, my lord?"

"Yes, thank you, Arwine," St. Cloud said. "Head back to the rectory and assure Mr. Fleming his sister is safe. We'll follow in a minute."

"Yes sir." The man turned his horse around and galloped back, the lantern's light bouncing beside him until it vanished in the darkness.

"D-don't you need the lantern?" Amanda stammered. Having the Earl of St. Cloud's arm around her waist was doing interesting things to her pulse.

Not to mention her heart.

He pulled his scarf from his neck and wrapped it around hers. Sitting in the circle of his arms, she could not escape his warmth spreading around her. "I grew up here, Miss Fleming," he said. "I can find my way home in the dark. And even if I couldn't, Socrates can. If we hurry, I'll make it to the Pembrokes just after Perdita does."

Recalling Lucy Pembroke's invitation this morning to him and Perdita, Amanda sighed. "Oh, dear. I've made you late for your dinner engagement."

"Not if we hurry." With one arm still around her waist, St. Cloud turned Socrates around, and moved him into a gallop. They rode in silence for several moments before Amanda worked up the courage to ask, "How is it that you came looking for me, my lord?"

"Your brother came to Heart's Ease with the news you hadn't returned from your afternoon ride. He said because of his near night blindness, he would be quite useless to help in the search and so—."

"He thought you would be the best choice," Amanda finished. "For who would know the area around here better than you?"

"I suppose so," he said matter-of-factly. "But there's another reason."

His warmth against her should have eased some of the tension from her body. Instead, it and the strength of his arm around her only served to keep her heart moving at a gallop nearly as fast as Socrates's own. "What would that be, my lord?"

"I think he thought as I too have only one sister, I would understand better than anyone his concern for your safety. You frightened him terribly, Miss Fleming. You should know that."

If he had yelled at her, or accused her of foolishness, she would have been able to stand it. But his voice's quiet accusation acted like a lance, striking her conscience with deadly precision and starting an ache in her heart. She would rather take a beating than hurt her twin.

They rode the rest of the way to the rectory in silence. The only sound other than her heart roaring in her ears was Socrates's hooves beating against the nearly frozen earth, sending a spray of snow to settle against them like a swatch of frozen lace.

And yet, there was no other place that Amanda would rather be. Incredibly, against all reason, and all their past encounters, Amanda was falling in love with Cameron Hunt. She only hoped that Lucy had the sense to accept his proposal of marriage as soon as her Aunt Adelaide arrived.

Too soon, even her eyes could make out the lights in the rectory window. Socrates's approach must have alerted Stephen of their approach, because the front door jerked opened and her brother burst out onto the front porch, and came down the front steps, followed by Thomas who held up a lamp.

And with them was Perdita. Behind Amanda, St. Cloud stiffened as he pulled Socrates to a halt by the steps and a waiting coach.

His coach. Even the horses didn't look happy and George's frozen expression had nothing to do with the falling temperature.

"Thank God," Stephen said, reaching up to help Amanda from the saddle. "I've been half out of my mind with worry."

"So have I!" Perdita pulled Amanda into a rib-bruising hug. "Wherever have you been?"

"Perdita, what are you doing here? You're supposed to be at the Pembrokes." St. Cloud slid from Socrates and glared at them, as if trying to decide which one of them had caused him the most trouble. George, an explanation if you please."

"Ask her ladyship, my lord." George's frown matched his employer's.

"I made him bring me." Perdita put in, returning St. Cloud's stony gaze with hauteur. "Did you think I was going to sit at the Pembrokes, sick to death with worry while waiting for you to arrive with news of Amanda?"

"I told Oakley to have George take you there and wait for me." Ice dripped from St. Cloud's tone.

"And I told George if he didn't bring me here to wait with Stephen, I would either saddle Bandit myself and ride over here, or I would walk." Perdita folded her arms over her chest. "He didn't have a choice. And so here I am."

"Can't argue with Miss Perdita when she sets her mind to do something, my lord," George called gloomily from his perch. "We all know that."

"Is Daisy here?" Amanda asked, desperate to change the subject. She unwound St. Cloud's scarf and gave it back to him.

"She showed up just after the earl and Mr. Arwine left,"

Stephen said, leading them back inside and shutting the door. "Perdita and I put her in the stable and gave her a good rub down and fed her. Amanda, what happened?"

Keeping her gaze on the floor, Amanda followed into the parlor with the St. Clouds right behind her. After they were seated, and Hamish joined Perdita on the loveseat, Amanda said," I dismounted to give Daisy a bit of a rest and fell asleep by a tree," she said. "I'm sorry, Stephen. I didn't mean to frighten you, or you either, Perdita. And I'm sorry I've made you late for your evening with the Pembrokes, my lord."

"Well, thank God you're all right," Stephen said, sinking against his chair. "My lord, could we convince you to stay for dinner? Mrs. Crawford has been keeping it hot."

"And we could tell you about the ideas Stephen and I discussed for the new Sunday school while we waited. We can talk about it over dinner," Perdita added. She turned adoring eyes on St. Cloud, who had gone to stand before the fireplace, his hands behind his back. "I knew if any one could find you Amanda, it was you, Cam."

"We have a previous invitation for dinner at the Pembrokes, Perdita," St. Cloud reminded her. He took out his pocket watch and consulted it. "If we leave now, we'll not be too late. I hope you had the courtesy to send word we would be detained?"

"Of course, I did," Perdita said crossly, fondling Hamish's ears. "And you know very well that the Henrys will be late. They're *always* late."

"But we are not," St. Cloud replied. "If you will please excuse us, Mr. Fleming?"

Stephen scrambled to his feet. "Thank you for your help, my lord. And please give my thanks to Mr. Arwine and George as well."

"They were only too happy to help," St. Cloud said, but Amanda was sure his steward and coachman would have preferred to stay inside near a fireplace rather than searching after a clergyman's misplaced sister.

"Yes," Amanda said. "Please give Mr. Arwine and George my thanks as well, my lord."

St. Cloud inclined his head before heading to the door. "I'll do that. Come, Perdita."

Sighing, Perdita kissed the top of Hamish's head and followed her brother into the hall. The front door clicked close and Stephen sank into his chair again. "Amanda? What did you think you were doing, riding alone?" Anger settled over his features, while frustration weighed down his usually gentle tone.

"I know, I know," Amanda said miserably. "I'm sorry, Stephen. Please don't scold me again. Once today was enough."

"I'm sorry, Mandy," he said, "but I was so terribly worried. I only have one sister. After all, who else would let me try out my sermons on them and let me know if I were getting it right?"

"There's always Hamish," she teased, her heart lightening at his gentler tone.

"Yes, but he's such a silent critic, if not for you, I'd never know if I were off the mark."

"And I've never been known for my silence, have I?" Amanda asked. "Now, I have some news that should make you feel better as well."

Her spirits rose at his happy expression as she described the triumvirate's agreement to come to tea to discuss Christmas traditions at All Souls.

"Mandy, that's splendid of you," Stephen praised, taking her hands and bringing them both to their feet. "I know the ladies are a bit stiff, but they've helped run things for so long before we arrived. Let's try not to upset them."

"It will be my Christmas present to you," Amanda teased as they walked into the dining room and sat at the table.

"And speaking of Christmas presents," Stephen said after Mrs. Crawford and Thomas had served them, "I haven't even begun my shopping yet. What do you say we go into Chastleford later this week and spend the day in the shops? Do us good to explore it and see what's there."

"I think that's a fine idea," Amanda agreed, glad to get away from the subject of the triumvirate. Unless

Stephen insisted, she was *not* going to buy presents for them.

But much later, lying in bed with Hamish snoring beside her, Amanda offered up a prayer, to not only try to not upset the triumvirate, but to not further annoy Cameron Hunt, the Earl of St. Cloud.

Chapter Ten

"So, shall we draw lots?" Allister Hunt flashed a smile around the breakfast table. "I'm itching to see which of us will be the one to represent the Hunt family in this year's Christmas race."

"You better wait for Perdita and our wives to come down to breakfast, old man, "Richard warned. "Gwenyth has already warned me. If we draw without them here, there will be the devil to pay all the way back to London. Wives, if there are any, must be present. That's the tradition, right, Cam?"

Falling asleep in the woods and forcing people to come look for her after dark. Ridiculous. What kind of woman does such a thing?

"What would he know about wives?" Allister argued. "The man's still a bachelor at almost thirty! Wives are as much a foreign territory to Cam as Outer Mongolia. No offense, Cam, but you can't deny it's true."

From the moment you've arrived, Amanda Fleming, you've managed to keep things here in Huntingdown spinning like a top. Heaven only knows what you'll do next.

"Cam's problem is he's too particular. All those beauties just dying to become his countess and he still can't settle on one. If we wait for Cam to choose a wife, our future children will be off at university," Richard said. "So is there ever to be a Countess St. Cloud, Cam? Don't keep us in the dark."

Like having me hold you in my arms again. Sitting there before me on Socrates, like a sylph, slender but strong, your scent branding itself on my skin. . .

"Cam, the library is on fire!"

"What?" Allister's shout pulled Cam out of his reverie, bringing him halfway out of his chair. His brothers' grins put him back. "Very funny," he said.

"Did you hear a single word we said?" Richard teased.

"Every last syllable," Cam retorted. "You were discussing the likelihood of my ever finding the most suitable bride to be my countess and that your children would all be at university before it happened. And Richard is right, Allister. We draw lots for the race at our own risk if the ladies aren't present."

Silence reigned for a moment. "Devil take it," Richard finally said. "How could we have forgotten that he always hears everything that's said, even when you think his mind is a thousand miles away?"

"Papa could do it too," Allister said ruefully. "Never could get anything past him either."

"Something you'd do well to remember." Cam reached for the coffee pot on the table and refilled his cup while silently thanking his late father for inheriting the ability to divide his attention and still never miss a thing. "And must I remind you that over the years I have won the race five times to both of you winning only twice?"

Richard winked at Allister. "Still the same old Cameron, modest to a fault."

"Just wait until he's married with children," Allister countered with a grin. "He'll be insufferable."

"And speaking of marriage, have you popped the question to Lucy Guest yet?" Richard put his elbows on the table and rested his chin in his hands. "Have we missed the reading of the banns or were you waiting for us?"

"Perdita said last night that Victor Graham and Thomas Osborne dined with you at the Pembrokes." Allister's broad grin made him look like a schoolboy with a secret to tell. "And that could only be for one reason. They're also interested in the fair Lucy. Do tell, Cam. How fared you against the competition? Did you shatter it completely or will you be searching about for another bride?"

"The gentlemen you mention arrived with their horses for the sleigh race," Cam said, filling his coffee cup again. "If you wanted to observe their interest in Miss Guest, you should have arrived in time to join us instead of after midnight when we were all in our beds."

Recalling last night at the Pembrokes, a satisfied warmth spread through him. In spite of Osborne and Graham's gentlemanly flirtation, and Lucy's ladylike reception of it, she made it clear that the gentlemen were wasting both their charm and their time. Her attention was fixed on Cam, and Cam only. Emmaline Pembroke's satisfied smile was a degree short of a smirk, and Pembroke all but pulled Cam into a corner to discuss Lucy's dowry.

But Lucy's great aunt Adelaide had still not arrived and Pembroke knew better than to permit anyone, even Cam, to propose before that. Lucy would have refused to consider it anyway, so what was the point?

Allister's scowl brought Cam back to the discussion at hand. "We didn't think it would snow all the way from before Guildford to Heart's Ease. It slowed us down considerably, which is why our wives are still in bed. And shouldn't we send for them? We always draw lots at nine o'clock sharp."

But Richard refused to concede the earlier point. "Is it to be Lucy, or not, Cam? Or would you have us believe that after all this time another beauty has caught your eye?"

"Good morning, everyone. Are we ready for the drawing of the lots?" Perdita's entrance thankfully delayed Cam from having to supply an answer to his brothers' Inquisition.

"Good morning, Perdita," he said. "You're looking well this morning."

"Hullo, Perdy," Allister greeted, using her childhood nickname. "You're doing your hair differently. Are you busy practicing your come-out curtsey?"

"Have you bankrupted us yet, choosing your debut wardrobe?" Richard teased. "Will there be any money left by next spring?"

"You shouldn't be so quick with your teasing," Perdita said demurely, taking her place at the table. "I looked in on both Rosalind and Gwenyth before coming downstairs and you are both commanded to bring them news of our racer as quickly as possible. Neither feels well enough to join us for the traditional drawing, but I suppose being with child might do that to a woman. At least they're not casting up their accounts."

"Perdita!"

She blinked at the trio of protesting voices. "What?"

"Language, Perdita," Cam said sternly. "Language!"

"Oh, very well," she said. "It is time, isn't it?"

The wall clock chimed out the nine o'clock hour in answer. When it finished, Cam reached for the silver bell next to his cup and rang it. As if waiting behind the door, Oakley entered and asked, "Is it time, my lord?"

"Yes," Cam said. "You may begin, Oakley."

The butler departed, only to return seconds later, carrying a small flat box. After he chose a spot in the corner, he said,

"Lady Perdita, if you would be so good as to assist me?"

"With pleasure," Perdita intoned. She went to join him and a series of whispers was exchanged. Then she returned to the table and cleared her throat.

"Gentlemen," she said, continuing in the same lofty tone. "You will recall the rules. Each of you will pull one of the small sticks from my hand," she said and held it out for them to see the small wooden sticks jutting up from her fist. "Hide it in your hand. Not until all the sticks are pulled, may you open your hand so we can compare and see who will be our racer. The one with the longest stick is the winner. Allister, since you are the youngest male, tradition dictates you will go first."

Allister grinned at his brothers and drew his stick. Perdita moved about the table to Richard, her expression as solemn as a novice taking her final vows. After Cam pulled his stick, Perdita opened her hand. "As you see, there are no more," she said. "Gentlemen, present your sticks!"

The brothers placed their sticks on the table side by side and Richard let out a whoop. "Strike me pink, I won!"

"Congratulations, Richard," Cam said. "It's been a while since you raced."

"Good job, Richard, " Allister added. "Now you can convince Gwenyth to let you buy that horse at Tattersall's you want. You'll just have to decide which one." It was a tradition that the winner had the full support of his other brothers with no complaints or whining. Their parents had detested whining.

The door opened and the housekeeper, Mrs. Oakley, appeared, trying unsuccessfully to hide her smile.

"Excuse me, Master Richard, Master Allister," she said. Your wives are asking for you. Somewhat stridently, I might add."

"I think that's the signal for us to leave and share your good news, Richard." Allister patted his lips with his napkin and rose. "We'll talk about the race later, Cam."

"We'll need to decide which of the horses to buy," Richard said, also getting to his feet. "Let's go for a short ride before we leave. Cam? Perdita? Will you join us?"

"If our wives will let us out of their sight for that long," Allister called over his shoulder, and a laughing Richard followed him into the hall.

"You're not still angry with me are you?" Perdita asked without preamble. "For going to the rectory last night while you were searching for Amanda?"

"I've never been angry with you longer than five minutes," Cam said gently. No one could stay angry long with Perdita. He filled her coffee cup and asked, "You're quite fond of Miss Fleming, aren't you?"

Perdita nodded. "I like her better than anyone I've ever met. She's fun and she doesn't seem to care too much what people think about her."

"Which could be a problem if she wants to marry a respectable man," Cam told her. "A lady's reputation as a lady is her dearest possession."

Good heavens. I sound like Father! Am I getting pompous before I turn thirty?

"She's a gentleman's daughter," Perdita countered, pouring cream into her coffee. "And there's nothing wrong with her reputation. Why don't you marry Amanda?"

Only massive self-control kept Cam's cup from falling from his hand to the table. "Perdita Louise Hunt," he said sternly. "I will thank you not to make such suggestions out loud or in public. Lucy and I have an understanding—"

"An understanding?" Perdita frowned as she uncovered the toast and put a piece on her plate. "What kind of understanding? Have you ever actually asked Lucy to marry you?"

"Perhaps expectation would be a better word," Cam amended. "And no, I have not asked Lucy to marry me. Not yet."

"But she's kept you waiting for three years."

"While she was at school," Cam reminded her. "As it was her dearest wish to attend the same finishing school her great-aunt Adelaide attended, I could hardly ask her to marry me until she finished."

"And now Lucy is the perfect lady," Perdita said crossly. "She's so perfect I'd be afraid to sneeze around her. She'd never even *think* about trying to ride astride or race with me—"

"Thank God for that," Cam interrupted. "Perdita—"

"—or make an Advent wreath for the church! Cam, Lucy's not any fun! Not like Amanda. Don't you like Amanda even a bit?"

"I knew sending you to that young ladies' seminary was a mistake," Cam muttered. "You've become far too outspoken and now *you're* giving *me* advice on who I should marry?"

"But Cam—"

"That's quite enough." Cam shoved his chair back and rose so quickly it toppled over. "Perdita, I am not going to discuss this with you. My personal affairs, including my pending engagement to Lucy, should she have me, are none of your, or anyone else's business. Is that quite clear?"

Perdita lowered her head. "Yes, Cam."

"Good. Now if you'll excuse me, I need to talk to the gardening staff about the decorations you want for the ball."

He had made it to the door when Perdita's voice stopped him. A voice filled with a newfound confidence, one obviously gained from her friendship with Amanda Fleming.

"You won't be happy if you marry Lucy," her voice accused. "She may be suitable, but you won't be happy."

Her words sent a wave of doubt rippling through his heart, and he almost turned back to argue with her again. A lone bead of sweat broke out on the back of his neck to travel past his collar.

Marry Amanda Fleming? Incredible. Outrageous. Impossible. The image of her racing toward him and Lucy, hat gone and hair flowing down her back crashed into his memory. A Viking princess indeed.

Then sense and logic returned. Perdita was a child, and he was the ninth Earl of St. Cloud. Earls do not marry the outspoken, independent and totally unpredictable sisters of clergymen.

Especially when they look like Viking princesses.

And with the weapons of logic and sense on his side, Cam continued out into the hall and to the hothouses.

****

"And so you see, Miss Fleming, we've everything for the Christmas Eve services well in hand," Mrs. Baker said proudly. "We three consider it our sacred Christian duty to keep things running smoothly at All Souls."

You mean keeping others off the Altar Guild and other positions at the church to insure that you will maintain your grip on things. Amanda's cheeks ached from forcing her lips to maintain a smile during tea, but she promised Stephen she would try to be nice to these women. She wasn't about to ruin his first Christmas at All Souls by making it his last.

So she would be nice to the powers of Tarwater, Baker and Hopewell even if it killed her.

"How very kind of you," she said, filling her visitors' cups once again. "I'm sure Mr. Smythe depended on you a great deal. Is there anything else we need to discuss about Christmas traditions at All Souls?"

"No, but my husband told me something very interesting last night," Mrs. Tarwater said. "And as he is the Senior Warden, he is in a position to know."

And of course he told you before he told Stephen. "Concerning All Souls?" Amanda said with as much innocence as she could muster. "May you share it with us?"

"Josiah Hawkins has decided to retire as verger."

This was not what Amanda had expected to hear. "But hasn't Mr. Hawkins been verger here for a very long time?"

"Too long if you ask me," Mrs. Baker chimed in. "He's nearly seventy and getting absentminded. Just imagine what might happen if he forgot to come to the service on Christmas Eve."

"How odd," Amanda said. "Stephen and I had lunch with Mr. Hawkins two days ago and he didn't mention it."

Karen Hall

"He only decided yesterday," Mrs. Tarwater said hastily. "He feels badly about leaving All Souls just before Christmas, but he received a letter from his daughter, asking him to come and live with her in Plymouth. She especially wants him there for Christmas."

Suspicion curled around the base of Amanda's spine. "But why didn't Mr. Hawkins tell Stephen himself?"

"Josiah and my husband have been friends for so long, it was just habit to tell him first." Mrs. Tarwater might have been explaining a very simple lesson to a stubborn child. "I'm sure Josiah will tell your brother sometime today. And Mr. Tarwater even has a suggestion for a replacement."

Recalling Hattie Nichols's description of how the vestry had dashed her grandson's dreams of being trained for verger, rang a warning bell in Amanda's head. "And who might that be?" she asked. "I'm sure Stephen will want to meet with him."

"My husband," Mrs. Hopewell said proudly. "And since Mr. Hopewell is on the vestry and attends church every Sunday, there is very little need for training. He's watched Mr. Hawkins perform his duties hundreds of time. I'm sure Mr. Hawkins can have him ready by Christmas Eve."

"I see." Excitement quickened Amanda's heart as an idea began to take shape in her mind. But she managed to smile at her guests and ask, "May I offer you some more cake?"

Chapter Eleven

Several days later.

"Are you sure you don't want me to wrap this one too, Miss?" The woman slid the second small, flat box across the counter and handed Amanda her change. "There isn't any charge to wrap them both."

"No, thank you," Amanda told her, slipping the boxes into her cloth shopping bag. Stephen desperately needed new gloves. These would make the perfect Christmas present and he could wear them during the sleigh race.

But she had also just done something outlandish, something a single lady should never do for a single gentleman of her acquaintance.

She had purchased a new pair of gloves for Cameron Hunt.

After all, she argued with herself as she left the men's haberdashery, she was partially responsible for his ruined gloves. Her and the rabbit. Hamish would get no blame. Hamish was a Scottish Terrier, and everyone knew terriers chased things.

So it wasn't as if she were buying St. Cloud a *gift*.

Recalling his irritated expression as he rose from the mud, Amanda's cheeks burned. Weeks ago, she would have laughed at the memory of his affronted dignity. But now? Oh dear.

Because now she was falling head over heels with the earl of St. Cloud. Any day now, she would be called upon to smile and wish him joy when his engagement to Lucy Guest was announced.

And she wasn't sure she could watch that without it breaking her heart. She just hoped her guess about St. Cloud's glove size was correct.

Withholding a sigh, she continued down Chastleford's High Street. Situated five miles from Huntingdown, it offered a larger selection of shops and specialty stores. This was the first time since taking up the living at All Souls that she and Stephen visited Chastleford. It was pretty enough, but she realized she much preferred Huntingdown's slower pace, and the beauty and quiet of its surrounding countryside. But then, she grew up in the countryside and always found city life to be wanting.

An ornately carved sign hanging over the sidewalk ahead, proclaimed the establishment below it to be Cardshaw's Books and Fine Things. The late morning sun hit the sign's gold letters giving them a lustrous sheen that tempted the viewer to enter.

And there in the shop's large front window was displayed another present she could give Stephen. Smiling, Amanda pushed open the door and entered.

"Good morning, Miss." A bearded man stepped from behind the counter and bowed.

"Laurence Cardshaw, at your service. Welcome to Cardshaw's Books and Fine Things. Is there something in particular I might help you find?"

"Yes, please," Amanda said. "I would like to purchase a copy of Southey's *Life of Nelson*, like the one you have on display."

"Oh, dear, I'm so very sorry." Mr. Cardshaw shook his head. "We've just sold our last copy."

"But the one in the window?" Amanda said, her excitement fading. "Surely you would be willing to sell that one?"

"I'm afraid we need to keep that one for display." Regret colored Mr. Cardshaw's tone. "The book has been so popular, we've not been able to keep it in stock."

"I wanted to purchase it for my brother for a Christmas present," Amanda said sadly. "He's so been wanting to read it, but with us just moving to the area, he simply hasn't had the time to purchase his own copy."

"I would be glad to take your order for the next shipment," Mr. Cardshaw offered. "But we would not have them until after Christmas."

"Then it would seem the only thing to do is to give the lady my copy."

Cameron Hunt emerged from the stacks, two volumes tucked under his arm. Immaculately turned out as always, it was amazing that even with Lucy Guest his

116

prospective bride how, he could have stayed a bachelor for so long. He was quite simply, breathtaking.

Somehow her brain remembered how to work and she curtsied. "Good morning, my lord. I hope I find you well?"

He bowed in return. "Very well, Miss Fleming," His baritone voice spread over her, warming her skin while his eyes' assessment only added to the throbbing of her pulse. "And yourself?"

"I am well," she said. "Stephen and I came into Chastleford to do some Christmas shopping. He's out buying a present for me, so of course I was told to make myself scarce and here I am."

"Perdita said the same thing," St. Cloud said. "She has George in attendance at some undisclosed location. And so, here I am. Did I hear you say you hoped to purchase Southey's *Life of Nelson* for your brother?"

Amanda's disappointment returned. "Yes. Stephen has wanted to read it for ages, so I decided it would be the perfect Christmas present. But its popularity is my undoing. Mr. Cardshaw says the next shipment will not be here until after Christmas."

"It's very hard to find copies in London as well," Mr. Cardshaw added. "I visited several bookstores there last week, but there wasn't a single copy to be had."

"Then there's only one thing to be done, Miss Fleming," St. Cloud said. "You must take my copy and give it to your brother."

"My lord!" Amanda was aghast. "I can't let you do that!"

He raised a single eyebrow. "Why not?"

"Because—because it's yours."

"And as such, I am free to do with it what I like. Mr. Cardshaw?"

"Yes, my lord?" Curiosity danced in Cardshaw's eyes.

"I insist you sell Miss Fleming the copy of *Life of Nelson* that I just purchased, please. Her brother is the new rector at All Souls in Huntingdown and regarded as a very fine scholar. You may apply the price of that to these." St. Cloud held up his two books.

"As you wish, my lord." Cardshaw's gaze traveled back to Amanda. "Is there anything else I might find for you, Miss Fleming?"

"Well," Amanda hesitated. "How very fortunate we should meet like this, my lord. I planned to buy Lady Perdita a book as well. Perhaps you might help me in my selection? That is, if you think she would enjoy a book."

The mention of Perdita brought a smile to St. Cloud's features. "A book would please her greatly, Miss Fleming. In fact, might I suggest these?" He handed her the two volumes."

118

"Oh, excellent choice," Amanda praised. *Pride and Prejudice* as well as *Sense and Sensibility*, both by the lady whose name is unknown to us. Has Lady Perdita not read them yet?"

"I don't believe so, but I have read them both and I think she's old enough to appreciate them," St. Cloud said. "You've read them?"

"Yes, and enjoyed them very much. Although," she laughed, "her descriptions of clergymen are not at all flattering."

"Ah, the repulsive Mr. Collins." St. Cloud made a face. "Perhaps the lady knows clergyman *very* well."

Amanda laughed at his dour expression. "But if you were planning on giving Lady Perdita these books—"

He cut off her off with a wave of his hand. "Miss Fleming, I have a vast number of other presents to give my sister this year. I think two novels about love from a lady friend would tickle her fancy like nothing else. She is supposed to meet me for refreshments at Sanford's in ten minutes. Would you and your brother care to join us?"

"Thank you, my lord." *Do I sound delirious with joy? Think of how Elinor if not Marianne would behave.* "I should enjoy that very much. Stephen and I also planned to meet at Sanford's."

"Then fate must have determined that we meet like this," St. Cloud said. "And it is never wise to tempt the Fates, or so the Greeks would have us believe. Shall we go?"

119

They went to the counter to pay for her purchases. Mr. Cardshaw placed St. Cloud's copy of *Life of Nelson* on the counter and Amanda sighed in pure pleasure.

"We will of course, credit your account, my lord," Mr. Cardshaw said. "Perhaps for another copy of the Southey?"

"Excellent idea," St. Cloud said. "Thank you."

"My biggest problem," Amanda told him, "will be not re-reading the Southey before Christmas and having Stephen find me with it."

Only the slightest widening of his eyes showed surprise at her words. "You have read *Life of Nelson?*"

"Yes," she said, taking the books from Mr. Cardshaw and adding them to her shopping bag. "In Stephen's last parish, there was an elderly gentleman whose eyesight was failing. He asked me to read it aloud to him, and I found myself fascinated by Mr. Southey's re-telling of the life of England's greatest naval hero. I know it's not what most ladies would choose to read, but I enjoyed it."

St. Cloud nodded and gave her a slight smile. "Then I hope you will contain your desire to read it again until after your brother reads it for the first."

He offered her his arm, and Amanda slipped her hand around it, enjoying the feel of its strength beneath the cloth. Outside the shop they walked to Sanford's in companionable silence. Once inside and seated at a table next to a front window, St. Cloud ordered and they sat back to wait for Perdita and Stephen. "Are you excited about your first Christmas at All Souls?" he asked.

Not nearly as excited as I am sitting here alone with you. At least we're in a public place. "Very much so," Amanda told him. "And are you excited about the upcoming race?"

He shrugged. "A bit. My brothers and I always draw lots to see which one of us will race. My middle brother, Richard, won this year. It would be unfair to have more than one St. Cloud enter."

"Why? Because you're all that good?" Amanda dared to tease. "Would you come in first, second and third?"

His smile could have melted the snows of Siberia. "Not to boast, but yes. We learned from the best."

Amanda put her hand over her heart in a display of mock admiration. "Truly all the other competitors must be in awe of your family's ability."

"The smart ones are."

"Oh, I nearly forgot!" St. Cloud's smile could do that to a girl. Amanda reached into her shopping bag, took out the unwrapped box and gave it to him. "This is for you, my lord."

His smile vanished as he stared at it, and then at her "What is this?"

"It's not a present," Amanda assured hastily. "If you open it, you'll understand."

He carefully removed the box's top and pulled apart the paper. "Gloves?" he asked.

"To replace the ones that were ruined when the rabbit scared Socrates and you lost your balance trying to control him," Amanda explained.

"You mean when I *fell* off of him. Miss Fleming, this wasn't necessary. It was an accident."

"I know that," Amanda said. "But perhaps if I had gone into the inn instead of walking Hamish, the accident wouldn't have happened."

He frowned. "I have plenty of gloves, Miss Fleming."

"I know that too," Amanda insisted. "But it's only right that I replace them."

"No, it isn't."

"Yes, it is."

"Miss Fleming, has anyone ever told you that you're stubborn and hard-headed?"

"Frequently." She lifted her chin and tried to ignore the pounding of her heart. "It's something I do well."

"So I see."

"Cam! Amanda!" Perdita called from the other side of the store. St. Cloud quickly put the glove box into his own shopping bag as Perdita hurried forward with Stephen a few paces behind.

"Stephen told me you were with him," Perdita said to Amanda, stopping at the table. "Isn't this wonderful?"

She waited until Stephen helped her sit and took his place, before asking, "Did you finish your shopping, Cam?"

"Very nearly," he told her. "And you?"

"'Very nearly,'" she pitched her voice in a perfect mimicry of his and they laughed. "I love Christmas, don't you, Amanda?"

"Yes," Amanda said. "It's my favorite time of year."

The waitress arrived, pushing a wheeled tea cart. After serving them, she left and Peridta acted as hostess.

"Are you nearly ready for the Winter Ball, Lady Perdita?" Stephen asked.

"I hope so," Perdita said, filling their cups. "I've looked over all the old plans my mother left. I want to make it perfect, the way she always did. I would want her and Papa to be proud of me."

A sheen of tears entered her eyes, making them brighter than usual and she put down the teapot. "I wish they were here to see this," she choked. "Sometimes I miss them so much."

Amanda put her hand over the younger woman's. "You will be the most celebrated hostess of the Christmas season," she declared. "Everyone who is not at the Winter Ball will be wild with jealousy at not being invited to it. The Patronesses of Almack's themselves will be so ashamed for not making the guest list, they will retire and go hide in the country!"

Perdita's half-sob turned into her now familiar laugh. "Oh, Amanda. Has anyone ever told you how funny and clever you are?" Amanda allowed her gaze travel to meet St. Cloud's. "Frequently," she said, not bothering to hide her smile.

"And do you have your gown for the Winter Ball ready as well?" Stephen asked.

"Cam and I are going to London tomorrow for my last fitting," Perdita said. "Amanda, do you have your gown?"

"I have one from a ball I attended last year."

"But you can't wear last year's gown!" Perdita gasped. "You shall come to London with Cam and me tomorrow and I'll have my modeste do one up for you."

"I can't afford a new gown," Amanda told her. "The one I had from last year will serve. It's very pretty."

"Oh, Mandy, go with them," Stephen said. "With what his lordship is paying me, we can well afford a new gown."

"Cam, tell her she must come with us," Perdita commanded.

"My sister has spoken, Miss Fleming," St. Cloud said. "You have no choice but to come with us to London tomorrow."

Amanda looked at the Hunt siblings. "You're sure it's not any trouble?"

"No trouble at all." Perdita said, picking up the pot again.

Being in London all day with you and your brother? Amanda's heart tumbled to her toes. *I have a feeling the trouble is only just beginning.*

Chapter Twelve

The next day.

"You've only been to London twice?" Perdita asked. "Cam, imagine that!"

Noting Miss Fleming's flushed cheeks, Cam said, "Miss Fleming has often lived in the country, Perdita. Perhaps she has had no occasion to travel there."

And now here she is in my best coach traveling with me to London. And I can hardly take my eyes off of her. Perdita, how do you convince me to agree to your madcap ideas?

"I'm sorry, Amanda," Perdita said quickly. "You're just so sophisticated, I thought you must have gone to London many times."

"No harm done, Perdita," Miss Fleming assured her. "And I do thank you again for this chance." She patted her reticule. "Stephen told me to buy whatever gown I wanted and to have the bill sent to him."

"Couldn't you convince him to come with us?" Perdita asked. "I think we'd all have such a cracking good time together. We could even take him to Cam's tailor, get him fitted out and then he'd be bang up to the knocker, even if he is a clergyman!"

"Perdita, please," Cam sighed. "Must you use such cant all the time? It isn't ladylike. What say you, Miss Fleming?"

He didn't dare look directly at Miss Fleming—who looked very well indeed in her mauve traveling suit—for to do so would have broken his example of brotherly control and sent him into uncontrolled laughter. Miss Fleming's tightly held lips were a marked contrast to her pretty face, but Cam could see them trembling in a brave effort to hold back her own mirth. Meeting her gaze while her eyes danced in a dangerous twinkle would have been the final blow.

"I think," she finally said, "that if you are going to use 'all the cant,' Perdita, you should only use it among your family. Some young men might not understand and as your brother correctly says, think you less of a lady. And you wouldn't want that."

"Thank you, Miss Fleming," Cam said. "You see, Perdita?"

"Oh, very well," Perdita grumbled good-naturedly. "I'll be a proper lady for the rest of the trip, just like Lucy would be."

At the mention of Lucy, Cam looked out the window at the approaching view of London. Considering his relationship with Lucy, traveling with Miss Fleming, even with Perdita, might not be "just the thing." Viscount Pembroke might have something to say about it. His wife certainly would.

But since she'd become friends with Miss Fleming, no matter how stubborn she might be, he'd never seen Perdita so happy. A new spark glowed within his beloved sister, and Miss Fleming clearly had lit it. The lady herself often radiated happiness, as if she carried her own internal flame of joy.

Careful. Cam heard the old voice of caution warn in his head. *Next thing you'll be reciting poetry, and then you're doomed.*

"——had to go see Squire Beecham about a horse and a sleigh for the race," he heard Miss Fleming say. "But he said perhaps another time we can all go together."

"I wonder who will win the race this year?" Perdita mused. "After all, we must get back the tradition of a St. Cloud winning. It's been three years since we had the trophy at Heart's Ease, but Richard will give them all a run for their money."

"Indeed he will," Cam agreed. "But I might have to go to Tattersall's to see about this horse he was boasting of the other day." *And also to see about the new horse I bought for your Christmas present.*

"Oh, I'd love to go to Tattersall's!" Perdita declared.

"Perdita, young ladies are *not* permitted at Tattersall's," Cam said sternly, fighting against a rising panic at the thought of his sister in that most masculine domain. "After we visit your modeste, I'll have George and Quinn drive you and Miss Fleming through Hyde Park or take you shopping, but you are *not* going to Tattersall's."

"I've only driven through Hyde Park once," Miss Fleming said helpfully. "There's no one I'd rather see it again with than, you, Perdita. And we must let everyone see Quinn in his new finery. Has he been your tiger long, my lord?"

"Why do you keep calling him, 'my lord,' Amanda?" Perdita looked first at Miss Fleming and then back at Cam. "You're friends, aren't you?"

A most becoming shade of pink spread over Miss Fleming's face and she lowered her gaze to her reticule. Silence filled the interior of the coach and remained for several moments until Cam cleared his throat and said, "I would be happy for you to call me by my given name, Amanda. That is if you have no objections, or think that your brother would not."

She lifted her gaze and her expression hit him with the force of a well-placed blow to the chin. "Thank you, Cameron," she said. "I don't think that Stephen will have any objections. But I do think it best that we only do so when we're in private. We wouldn't want people to think we were being overly familiar."

"I quite agree," Cam said. "Look, we're coming into town."

The horses picked up speed and for the next hour, at Cam's direction, they made a tour of London, with Cam pointing out the sites. It was something Cam had done many times over the years with visitors and friends from out of town, a tour he could give in his sleep.

But today for some reason, his pulse beat a little bit faster. It was almost as if he was giving the tour for the first time. But then, in a way he was.

It was the first time he was giving the tour to Amanda Fleming. Her eyes sparkled and excitement added a flush to her skin as he pointed out the sights. She shivered in mock terror as he described the horrors of the Tower of London and some of its victims, and laughed at his not quite respectful imitation of the Prince Regent. They were still laughing when they arrived at Carey's Fine Fashions off of Bond Street. Inside, no less than Mrs. Carey herself waited for them.

"My lord St. Cloud," she greeted with a smile and a curtsey. "And Lady Perdita! Welcome once again."

"This is my friend, Amanda Fleming," Perdita introduced. "She's come to look for a gown for the Winter Ball. Can you help her?"

"Perhaps," Mrs. Carey said as her staff came forward to take their coats. "If you'll come with me, Lady Perdita, I have your gown nearly ready. My lord, we won't be but a moment."

Cam led Amanda to a group of chairs and a table. When they were seated, she turned to look at him. "Thank you again, my lord, for this opportunity," she said, falling back into her usual formality. "It was most kind of you and Lady Perdita to invite me."

"I think you may have noticed by now, Miss Fleming," Cam said, "that it is nearly impossible to say 'no' to Perdita. Thank heavens she's not become a conceited little chit, for we've all spoiled her. And yet, she's the most unspoiled of souls."

"I know," Amanda said. "I've no doubt she will be a diamond of the first water next Season and the marriage proposals will follow hard and fast."

The thought of Perdita leaving Heart's East and Huntingdown must have shown on Cam's face, because Amanda said quickly, "I've upset you. I'm sorry."

"Not at all." Cam's fingers gripped the ends of the chair as a tightness gathered in his heart. "I must prepare myself for the day that Perdita will wed and leave us."

"Are your brothers as devoted to Perdita as you are?"

Her gentle tone erased some of Cam's tension and his grip relaxed. "Yes. Although I've them to blame for teaching Perdita to be such a bold rider. But you are quite correct. Perdita will take London by storm. It's only right she should find a suitable husband and marry well. But as she is my only sister, part of me wishes she would stay with us forever. Your brother would certainly understand."

"What do you think, Cam? Amanda?" At Perdita's question, Cam turned his head and then slowly got to his feet.

Hope shown in Perdita's face as she stood before them. Her pale, pink ball gown was simple yet elegant, and transformed the normally very pretty Perdita into a beauty that quite literally took Cam's breath away. He opened his mouth to speak and then closed it.

"Perdita, it's beautiful." Amanda's words supplied Cam's thoughts. "*You're* beautiful."

"Yes indeed," Cam managed to put his thoughts into words. *I'll have to hire security guards to be sure some buck doesn't carry you off to Gretna Green before I find you a proper husband.*

"I'll have to take it in a bit, here and there." Mrs. Carey had joined them and her brows drew together. "Have you lost weight, Lady Perdita?"

"The way she eats?" Cam asked. "I think not."

Perdita swatted him with the back of her hand. "Beast," she accused. "Mrs. Carey, I know the ball is soon, but can you make a gown for Amanda?"

"A *new* gown? In such a short time?" Mrs. Carey frowned and looked at Amanda. "I have so many other ladies' orders to finish, and even with all my girls working throughout the day, I couldn't guarantee I could have a new gown ready in time for the Winter Ball."

"That's all right," Amanda said quickly. "I have a gown from last year that would be perfectly suitable."

"Wait!" Mrs. Carey snapped her fingers. "I think I have an idea. There's a lady who has just returned several gowns and I think one of them just might suit Miss Fleming."

"Why did this lady bring them back?" Perdita demanded. "I won't have Amanda taking an ugly gown. She's too pretty to wear an ugly gown."

"Not at all, Lady Perdita," Mrs. Carey soothed. "If his lordship won't mind me saying so, the lady's husband discovered she had outstanding gambling debts and made her bring back half a dozen dresses so she could pay what she owed the tables. They're all quite lovely, and if one of them fits, and she likes it, I'll reduce the price for Miss Fleming."

"Go try one on then, Amanda," Perdita urged. "But not pink, please. I'd hate for people to think we were competing."

Miss Fleming smiled and followed Mrs. Carey into the back of the store. Perdita slowly walked around the large viewing room, as if testing how the gown felt, even stopping twice to practice a curtsy. At last she returned and sat in the chair next to Cam and looked at him, the hope still on her face. "Do you really like my gown?"

"If you like it, dearest, then that is all that is important," Cam said. But seeing a frown crease her forehead, he added, "Miss Fleming was right, Perdita. You look beautiful."

"Well now, Lady Perdita. What do you and the earl think of your friend's choice?" Mrs. Carey's voice signaled her return with Miss Fleming. Cam looked up and for a moment, surprise kept him in his chair. Then, still staring, he rose.

Like Perdita's, Miss Fleming's short-sleeved town was simple but elegant and gorgeous. The pale green silk shimmered like sunlight on the water. The bodice was low enough to be fashionable but still modest. Lace edged the sleeves and underneath the lacy overskirt dozens of tiny white flowers were stitched onto the fabric and the image of her at their first meeting leapt into Cam's memory. Amanda Fleming was a water-sprite come to life.

She slowly turned, the silk clinging lovingly to her slender body, and Cam swallowed down the lump in his throat. Gone was the image of the wild, Viking princess on her horse, leaving behind this delicate, fey creature.

I don't think it needs even a nip and a tuck," Mrs. Carey said, patting the dress. "It looks as if it were made just for you, Miss Fleming. A perfect fit, if I do say so myself. What say you, Lady Perdita? My lord?"

"Oh, Amanda," Perdita breathed. "You look like something out of fairy-tale! All you need is handsome prince to take you away. Your brother will be so pleased, won't he, Cam?"

A shimmering light entered Amanda Fleming's eyes, eyes that sought his approval, and one Cam would give if could just get the words past his throat.

"You look very well indeed, Miss Fleming," Cam said solemnly. "You'll have no shortage of partners at the ball."

"Thank you, my lord," she said. "Thank you, Perdita." Turning to Mrs. Carey, she added, "I'll take it if you're sure the lady will not return and ask for it."

"Ha!" Mrs. Carey exclaimed. "That's not likely."

"Very well, then. If you will all excuse me, please?" Miss Fleming headed for the dressing area.

"You see, Cam?" Perdita said happily. "I knew bringing Amanda to London was a good idea. She and I will both shatter hearts at the Winter Ball. Just you wait and see!"

Watching Miss Fleming vanish behind the curtain and into the safety of the dressing area, a strange heaviness gathered around in Cam's chest. "You will indeed, dearest," he said at last. "You will indeed."

Chapter Thirteen

Saturday before the Third Sunday of Advent

"My lord St. Cloud. A word if you please!" Wilfred Hopewell burst into Cam's study without so much as a knock on the door.

"Forgive me, my lord," A tight-faced Oakley managed to get past the angry Hopewell and plant himself like one of Heart's Ease ancient oaks in front of Cam's desk. "I did not tell you his lordship was home." He addressed Hopewell in the tone that had put terror into a generation of footmen in training and should have made Hopewell shiver in his boots.

"It's quite all right, Oakley." Cam shoved aside the final proposed menus for the Winter Ball and rubbed his temples. Even though they had left London well before dark yesterday—after he finalized the purchase of the new horse for Perdita at Tattersal's—it had started to drizzle, and the temperature dropped. By the time they were halfway home, the ice on the roads slowed the return to Heart's Ease to a near crawl. Never had the familiar journey seemed so long or exhausting. Sleep should have come quickly and easily, but it did not.

For every time he turned over, Amanda Fleming's image in a green ball gown danced before Cam's eyes, keeping sleep as far away as the moon.

"I think I can guess what this is about," Cam said.

"Oakley, would you please wait outside and be prepared to assist

Mr. Hopewell back to his carriage when I call?"

Oakley's lips curved into a grin of delighted malice. "Very good indeed, my lord. Yell if you need me." Then he scowled at the still fuming Hopewell. "You watch yourself," he warned. "Remember to whom you're speaking."

The door had hardly shut behind him when Hopewell leaned over and put his hands on Cam's desk. "That man you hired to be rector has appointed Arthur Nichols as verger! A tenant's grandson!"

"You mean Mr. Fleming?" Cam picked up his quill and ran his fingers over it. "That rector?"

"Tarwater told me *I* could have that position!" Hopewell snapped. "And that there Mr. Fleming goes and gives it to—"

"Arthur Nichols. Yes, I know. It is one of the rector's duties to appoint someone for verger as he sees fit," Cam said dryly. "Not the Senior Warden. If Mr. Fleming feels Arthur Nichols is qualified to be verger, I see no problem with his decision."

"But you gave Fleming the living at All Souls!" Hopewell argued. "You have the right to—"

"I may have given Mr. Fleming the living at All Souls, but I have no authority to dictate to him who he appoints to be verger or sexton or any other position at the church." Cam pulled the menus back. "If there is nothing else, Mr. Hopewell, I really need to continue preparing for the Winter Ball. Good day to you."

He lowered his head in dismissal but from under his eyelids watched Hopewell's visage turn from bright red to purple. The man hesitated, then turned on his heel and exited the room, slamming the door. Raised voices in the hall indicated Oakley was using Hopewell's bad manners as an excuse to exercise his authority to give Hopewell a lesson in manners. Another door slammed and Cam began silently counting. He had only reached five when the study door opened and Oakley came inside. "Will you be needing anything, my lord?" he asked. "Some coffee? A brandy? Or perhaps a whiskey?"

"Only if you'll have one with me," Cam said. Oakley enjoyed spirits on rare occasions, but in all the years he had worked at Heart's Ease, Cam had never seen him in his cups.

"It's a bit early in the day, my lord," Oakley said. A smile hovered around his mouth as he added, "Has Mr. Fleming really appointed Arthur Nichols as verger at All Souls?"

"Were you listening at the door, Oakley?"

The butler stood even straighter. "Certainly not, my lord. But you'll have to admit one can always hear anything Mr. Hopewell has to say without any problem at all."

Cam chuckled. "True enough. Do you have any objection to Mr. Fleming's decision?"

"No, my lord. Arthur Nichols is a hard-working, honest young man. If he'd been born a gentleman, he might have taken holy orders. And it's nice to see—"

He stopped, as if trying to decide if he should continue his statement. Cam waited, and when his servant still hesitated, he prompted, "Nice to see what, Oakley?"

"It's nice to see that someone recognizes that one doesn't have to be one of the gentry or the ton to help out at All Souls," Oakley said. "Arthur Nichols will do the job well and make us proud. I'm glad you offered Mr. Fleming the living there, my lord. He's a breath of fresh air, and if I may be so bold to say, so is his sister."

More like a whirlwind, stirring up trouble every time I turn around. "I think, Oakley, that after dealing with Mr. Hopewell, I could use a pot of strong tea after all."

"Very good, sir. Are you at home to anyone else?"

"No." And assigning Amanda Fleming to the back of his thoughts, Cam took up the menus for the Winter Ball.

****

"You mark my words, Amanda Fleming is behind this," Amelia Baker fumed. "The nerve! She probably went to her brother after asking us to tea to ask for advice on Christmas at All Souls and convinced him to appoint Arthur Nichols as verger! It's a deliberate insult to us. I've a good mind to write to the bishop about it."

"It's unheard of!" Grace Hopewell wailed, twisting her handkerchief into a rope. "A tenant's son being appointed as verger! How can I show my face at All Souls? Everyone knows that your husband promised Wilfred that he would be verger, Cecily! He's so angry that he's threatening to go to another church!"

"Oh, stop sniveling, Grace," Cecily said, rising from her chair to pace the length of her parlor. "You sound like a girl who's just been denied entrance to Almacks. This is Amanda Fleming we're talking about, not a member of the Royal Family! I've dealt with her kind before. Let me think."

The other women watched Cecily continue to pace before the window. "Writing to the bishop won't help. He'll just say it's Fleming's choice. But you're right, sister. I've no doubt that little Miss Busy-Body Fleming went straight to her brother after our tea at the rectory to suggest he appoint Arthur Norris verger instead of your husband, Grace. What else would have given him the idea?"

"Wicked, deceitful, girl," Grace whined. "Who does she think she is?"

"I don't know what the Earl was thinking, giving a living to such a young unmarried man," Amelia complained. "It's a shame that the earl seems so fond of Mr. Fleming. He's hardly likely to dismiss him unless he did something so outrageous they would forced to leave."

"And so many of the families seem to like Miss Fleming," Grace added. "Getting people excited about that Sunday school, or putting out Advent wreaths without even asking us, the Altar Guild! Miss Fleming is a troublemaker!"

"You're still upset because she asked Hattie Nichols to mend the altar linens instead of you," Amelia said. "Though much as I hate to say it, Hattie did do a good job."

"Are you siding with Amanda Fleming now?" Grace whined again. "It's my job to mend the linens, not anyone else! Amanda Fleming is a troublemaker !"

"Say that again, Amelia." Cecily said abruptly.

"I said Grace was still upset—"

"No, before that." Cecily turned and crossed the room to sit across from them. "About Stephen Fleming doing something so outrageous the earl would have to dismiss him and they would be forced to leave Huntingdown."

"But Cecily," Amelia said. "Mr. Fleming's conduct has been beyond reproach since his arrival. It's Miss Fleming's doings that have us upset. And as much as

I hate to say it, she hasn't exactly caused a scandal. Not a real one."

"Perhaps." Cecily tapped her chin in thought. "But it would only take the suggestion of a *possible* scandal to make them leave. You know how St. Cloud dislikes scandal."

The other two women stared at her in open-mouthed astonishment. "Cecily," Amelia said at last. "You can't do something to anger St. Cloud. It would ruin all of us!"

"I have no intention of any of us being ruined." Cecily sat back and smiled at her sister and friend. "Do you remember what Lady Perdita told us the night we dined at the Pembrokes? That they were late because Miss Fleming had gone missing and St. Cloud went to look for her. . ."

****

The Third Sunday in Advent

"Oh come, all ye faithful. . ." Beside Amanda, Hattie Nichols dabbed at her eyes as she watched Arthur light the third candle in the suspended Advent wreath and the choir sang the traditional hymn as they processed in. Perdita's soprano soared as she sang the descant and the choir took their places.

The church was far more crowded than the week before. People sat nearly shoulder to shoulder and

Amanda guessed the surge in attendance was due to Stephen appointing Arthur to be verger. Word of it had gotten out the day she went to London with the St. Clouds, and had spread like wildfire in the surrounding countryside.

And judging from the joy on not only Arthur's thin face, but Mrs. Nichols's too, naming Arthur verger was the right thing to do. From under her bonnet, Amanda flickered a look at the ladies of the triumvirate and their husbands. The three couples sang the words to the old hymn with gusto, their expressions suggesting nothing but joy for the season and not a care in the world more than what they might have for the midday meal.

And considering her encounters with the ladies, that made Amanda nervous. Mr. Hopewell, Stephen told her, had been very angry at not being named verger. Yet, here he was, singing away, one arm around his wife, who sent Amanda a smile. Amanda's pulse hitched a bit. The game, as Shakespeare told them long ago, was definitely afoot.

Don't be so suspicious, she scolded herself, turning her attention to Stephen's sermon. He urged them to remember the command to 'love thy neighbor as thyself', not just at this time of year, but all year long and that 'one's neighbor' meant everyone.

Lord, help me to remember that the triumvirate are my neighbors too, even if I don't like them. Give me a Christmas heart and not the suspicious one your very unworthy servant currently possesses. Amen.

At the coffee hour, Amanda watched people, including the triumvirate and their husbands, congratulate Arthur, and her sense of guilt increased. Perhaps the spirit of the season had finally touched their hearts.

Now all she had to do was make it through the week's activities and the Winter Ball. She looked around the room and spotted Lucy Guest and her parents talking to Perdita and St. Cloud. Funny how her brain, depending on the circumstances, could change which of his names she used when thinking of him. Perdita had told her at the last planning meeting for the new Sunday school that Lucy's great-aunt Adelaide was expected any day, and then Cam could approach the viscount about marrying Lucy.

"She's going to settle a great deal of money on Lucy," Perdita explained to Amanda. "And Lucy says she won't do it if she's not consulted on who Lucy marries as well."

Lord, I know it's Christmas, but could you somehow delay Lucy's Aunt Adelaide until after the holidays?

"Amanda!" Perdita called and beckoned to her from across the room.

Plastering on a smile she didn't feel, Amanda crossed the room to join them.

Chapter Fourteen

The day before the Winter Ball.

"The devil take it." Cam stared at the letter from Martins, his steward at Hope Springs, his estate in Dowling, a village outside of Guildford and a good five hour drive from Huntingdown. "Martins thinks he's dying and 'wants to see me one last time.'"

Oakley stifled a laugh with a cough. "How many times has he claimed this since you became St. Cloud, my lord? Two? Three?"

"This will make four. But this time he wants me to bring Mr. Fleming. Listen to this, Oakley." Cam leaned back in his desk chair and adopted Martins's slightly nasal voice. 'Having been told of the talented young clergyman to whom you gave the living at All Souls, I beseech you to bring him with you as quickly as possible, my good lord, so I may make my final peace with you and God.'"

This time Oakley couldn't stop his laughter. "He sounds as though he could give Edmund Keen's Shylock at the Lyceum a run for his money. Is that Shakespeare he's quoting, my lord?"

145

"No, damn all, it's his own." Cam folded the letter and dropped it onto the desk. "And just like our late, unlamented Mr. Smythe, Martins's sense of timing is abysmal. I suppose I have no choice but to go to Hope Springs and take Mr. Fleming with me. I hope he has his Christmas Eve sermon ready."

Oakley's eyebrows drew together. "Aren't you supposed to dine at the Pembroke's again this evening, my lord?"

"Yes," Cam sighed, pulling pen and paper forward. "I best send Quinn 'round with notes to them and Mr. Fleming. Ask Higgens to come downstairs, please, and then ask George to get the smaller of the traveling carriages ready."

After the notes were dispatched with Quinn, and packing instructions given to Higgens, Cam rose and walked to stare into the flames crackling in the fireplace. Outside, a granite sky covered the horizon and a steady wind beat against the mullioned windows. Snow was coming. Cam sighed. He just hoped he'd make it back in time for the Winter Ball. Why did Martins have to choose today to think he was dying?

Beginning with last Sunday, the past week had passed in a flurry of activities, involving Cam and Perdita in every one of them. Visiting tenant families and distributing their gifts, judging cattle and baking competitions took up their days while invitations to parties, dinners, and heaven help them, building snow forts by moonlight took up their evenings.

And at every one of them, Lucy was there, looking more and more beautiful. As if by some unspoken agreement by their hosts, Lucy and Cam were always seated near each other at dinner and at cards, or put on the same teams for charades, not to mention appointing Cam page-turner for Lucy when she played the piano-forte and sang. A gentle conspiracy seemed to be brewing to hurry Cam's proposal to her along, and it was nearly impossible to miss the winks and nods exchanged. The viscountess was nearly giddy with delight and her husband's smile was one of smug self-congratulation. Their daughter to marry an earl! Cam could just imagine the announcement in *The Times*.

But always in the background was Amanda Fleming. A strangely subdued Amanda Fleming. It was as if she had reigned in her natural exuberance, and dimmed the light that always seemed to shine from her. Cam found himself almost missing their verbal sparring. Her quiet behavior was a little unsettling,

But then around Perdita, anyone might appear quiet. When not at the church rehearsing her solo for the Christmas Eve service, his sister spent a great deal of time at the rectory with the Flemings. She would return home, bubbling with excitement about their many plans, and what things she and "Amanda and Stephen" hoped to do in the spring. Cam had never seen Perdita so happy.

A quick knock brought in both Quinn and Higgens to announce that Mr. Fleming would be ready to travel in a less than an hour's time and that Cam's single piece of luggage was ready to be stowed in the carriage.

****

"Mrs. Tarwater, Hopewell and Baker are asking to see you, Miss Fleming," Alice announced from the library door.

Surprised, Amanda put her book on the table and glanced at the clock. It was too late to invite the ladies to luncheon without giving Mrs. Crawford extra work in addition to what she was doing to help prepare for tomorrow night's Winter Ball, and far too early for tea.

Besides, Perdita had sent 'round a note, inviting her to spend the night at Heart's Ease. A sudden summons had taken St. Cloud, and Stephen with him, to another St. Cloud estate, and Perdita didn't want to be alone the night before the Winter Ball.

Unease began to creep along her skin. The triumvirate had never called before without sending word first, and this sudden appearance was out of character for women who had mastered the art of always doing exactly what was expected and doing it correctly.

And now here they were without invitation or warning. Unexpectedly, Amanda shivered, but managed to say calmly, "Please show them in."

Alice curtsied and quickly ushered in their guests before closing the door behind her. Amanda stood and gave them what she hoped was a welcoming smile. "Good afternoon, ladies. This is a pleasant, if unexpected, surprise. Won't you please be seated?"

"We won't stay long," Mrs. Tarwater said without preamble. Behind her, Mrs. Hopewell and Mrs. Baker stood at rigid attention, their expressions sullen. Amanda's sense of foreboding turned her skin cold, and her fingers curled against her palms. "Is there a problem? Something at All Souls?"

"In a matter of speaking," Mrs. Baker said stiffly.

"Oh dear," Amanda said. "Stephen isn't here right now. He had to go with the earl to check on a servant at Hope Springs."

"We know. My husband saw him in St. Cloud's carriage as they left Huntingdown," Mrs. Tarwater said. "Miss Fleming, it has come to our attention that there has been some talk in town about your brother and Lady Perdita."

Amanda blinked. "What on earth would anyone have to say about them?"

"That they have been alone together on more than one occasion," Mrs. Hopewell said primly. "As have you and the earl."

"But they were always here or at church!" Amanda protested. "Working on the plans for the new Sunday school! And when were the earl and I alone together?"

"The night you went missing—or supposedly went missing," Mrs. Hopewell's tone insinuated so much more. "The two of you came back together alone."

She pronounced *alone* as if it was the newest deadly sin and Amanda nearly choked on the bile that rose in her throat. "My horse ran away," she said, knowing already any explanation would be useless. "Stephen asked the earl to try to find me."

Mrs. Baker sniffed her disapproval. "Odd that a brother wouldn't assist in the search."

Rage and fear drove Amanda's heart into a gallop. "Stephen is nearly as blind at night as I am," she choked out. "There's no possible way he could have helped look for me."

"So you say," Mrs. Tarwater said. "Perhaps you and your brother concocted a plot to force the Hunts to marry the both of you. Perhaps that's why you came here in the first place."

"And it would be a shame," Mrs. Hopewell added, "if his lordship's pending engagement to Lucy Pembroke were to fall through because of your being alone with him. Not to mention what it might do to Lady Perdita's expectations because she was alone with your brother, not only while the earl searched for you, but all the other times at the church. Imagine the scandal."

"And I heard from Mr. Cardshaw himself when I went to his shop to buy a book for my daughter, that St. Cloud gave you a book he already purchased," Mrs. Baker said, obviously relishing Amanda's discomfort. "Mr. Cardshaw is such a gossip. I'm surprised word hasn't gotten back to Pembroke and his wife. Giving a gift to a lady who is not a family member."

"But the servants were here," Amanda returned to her defense of Perdita and Stephen. "They—"

"Can be bribed to say and do anything," Mrs. Baker said smugly. "Your brother is being paid quite handsomely by the earl, and could afford to silence your staff with a handful of silver if needed."

Her unveiled accusation hit Amanda with the force of a blow across the face. "This is about me, isn't it?" she whispered. "About me asking Mrs. Nichols to repair the altar linens, starting a Sunday school and asking Stephen to consider appointing Arthur Nichols verger instead of Mr. Hopewell."

"You don't really belong here, Miss Fleming," Mrs. Hopewell said. "You've been nothing but trouble since you arrived. All

Souls got along without you and your brother very well. He's a young man. Finding another position shouldn't be too hard. I believe I heard you say he had been offered a teaching position at his college at Oxford before accepting the living at All Souls. Perhaps he should go there."

Amanda's head reeled at the suggestion. "But Stephen loves it here at All Souls. If anyone leaves, it should be me."

"Just like you had to do at your brother's last two positions?" Mrs. Tarwater's voice held a silky menace. "Because of the trouble you caused there? Ah, I see from your expression I've hit the mark. I've been doing a bit of correspondence, you see. St. Cloud couldn't have the living at All Souls vacant at Christmas, so perhaps he just chose the first person available. It didn't matter if the man had a sister who was a known troublemaker. Imagine the scandal that might cause if the members of All Souls learned about your behavior at the other churches. The viscount is such a stickler for propriety he might object to his only daughter marrying the man who chose such a rector. What would Lucy's great-aunt Adelaide, the Dowager Duchess of Clairfield say about that?"

Dread filled Amanda's heart. "I didn't know her great-aunt was a duchess," she whispered.

"No? Lady Perdita didn't mention it? After spending all that time with St. Cloud?" Mrs. Tarwater affected a look of surprise. "How very interesting. And what might such a scandal do to Lady Perdita's first Season?"

Amanda bowed her head. "You win, Mrs. Tarwater," she choked. "At least allow Stephen to conduct the Christmas Eve and Day services. Leaving before then would be a scandal in itself. Please. We'll be gone by New Year's Day, I promise."

"See that you are," Mrs. Baker ordered.

"Then my husband can be appointed verger," Mrs. Hopewell added, not bothering to hide her glee. "The very idea of appointing a tenant's grandson is outrageous!"

"Now, now, Grace, that's enough." Mrs. Tarwater's smile of victory held nothing but venom. "I knew Miss Fleming was a sensible young woman and would see reason. She would never want harm to come to Lady Perdita or St. Cloud, would you Miss Fleming?"

"Of course not," Amanda said woodenly, fighting to keep such images out of her head.

"I'm glad you see it our way," Mrs. Tarwater said. "Thank you, Miss Fleming. We'll see ourselves out."

They left, and Amanda stumbled back to the loveseat and sat, just before her knees gave way. Nothing at Good Shepherd or St. Barnabas could have prepared her for this kind of treachery. How would she explain it to Stephen?

But they would have to leave. She would never, never allow Perdita's future happiness to be jeopardized by three power hungry harpies. Or Stephen's, for that matter.

Or Cameron Hunt's. She bowed her head as sorrow gathered in her heart. How could she have fallen so completely in love with him? Better to leave before being forced to watch him marry Lucy Guest. Perhaps there was wisdom in the triumvirate's treachery after all.

"Excuse me, Miss Fleming, but you seem to be very popular this morning." Alice's voice yanked Amanda's attention away from despair and she turned toward the door. "Yes?"

The housemaid came forward, carrying a small envelope. "This just came from Heart's Ease, Miss. And they've sent a carriage for you."

"Oh, Lord." Amanda offered up a hasty prayer as she tore open the envelope. *Please let nothing have happened to Stephen and Cameron.*

Inside there was only the briefest of messages from Perdita, which did nothing to ease Amanda's fears. *I need you. Please come. P.*

Still praying, Amanda grabbed her coat from the rack in the corner, shoved her arms into it as she dashed for the front door and out to the Hunt's waiting carriage.

Chapter Fifteen

"Perdita, what happened?" Amanda asked, handing her coat to a worried-looking Oakley. He gave her a brief nod and closed the drawing room door as Amanda went to join her friend who sat on the sofa before the fire. The younger girl promptly burst into tears, sobbing into her hands.

Terror seized Amanda's heart, but she gently pulled Perdita's hands from her face and said, "Perdita, talk to me. What has happened? Have your other brothers and their wives not arrived yet?"

"No," Perdita sobbed. "Richard and Allister are in London, finishing their Christmas shopping, and won't be back until tomorrow. And they wouldn't know that Cam and Stephen had to go to Hope Springs and *they* won't be back until tomorrow! And the Winter Ball is tomorrow night! Oh, Amanda, what am I going to do?"

"First you're going to tell me what has happened," Amanda coaxed. She put an arm around her friend's waist. "Surely between us we can make it right."

Taking a handkerchief from her pocket, Perdita dried her eyes and then blew her nose with a less than ladylike gusto. "That—" she pointed at a large open box on the table—"is what's happened."

What else could possibly go wrong? Holding back her sigh of resignation, Amanda went to the table to pull aside the folds of tissue paper and peer inside in box. "My word!" she gasped. "What on earth is it?"

"It's supposed to be my gown for the Winter Ball." Perdita's voice trembled.

"But it's—it's—"Amanda picked up the gown with her fingertips—"it's *orange*. Bright orange."

"I know!" Perdita wailed. "I can't wear that to the ball! I look *terrible* in orange! They've sent the wrong gown!"

"Oh, dear." Amanda let the gown fall back into the box and rejoined her friend. "I don't suppose we could send it back?"

"It came from London, remember?" Perdita gulped. "There's not enough time to send it back and even if we did, what if they don't have my gown? They've probably sent it to someone else, and it's so beautiful whoever has it won't want to give it back. Oh, Amanda. What am I going to do?"

She began to cry again, and for a moment, Amanda longed to join her. Her earlier meeting with the triumvirate left her bruised, heart and soul. The thought of being forced to leave Huntingdown because of their selfish concerns for keeping their power nearly brought her to tears. In Huntingdown, Amanda finally found a way to fit in as the rector's sister—or so she thought. And now that would to be taken away from her.

But today was not about Amanda. She would not give those old tabbies even the slightest chance to hurt Perdita. An idea began to form and she smiled.

"I'll tell you what we'll do." Amanda took Perdita's hands and rose, bringing the girl to her feet. ""We're going to be sure that you are the belle of the ball. Let's go."

****

"Whatever in the world is taking her so long?" Cam stared up the long staircase as he paced the foyer.

"Oh, for heaven's sake, Cam," Gwenyth scolded. "This is almost as important as making one's bow. Perdita will be down in a moment."

"I don't understand why she wouldn't let you or Rosalind help her dress," Cam argued. Perdita had been secretive, almost furtive since his return from Hope Springs that afternoon, not helping his bad mood at all. Martins of course had not died, but merely suffered from acute indigestion after eating a questionable meal of boiled mutton—a situation that could have been resolved by the local surgeon.

And even though his staff at Heart's Ease could plan and execute the Winter Ball without his help, Cam had not liked leaving Perdita. It was her first one, and he should have been here, not running off to wait for Martin to realize he would be among them for a good while longer. Servants. Sisters. It could turn a man's hair gray.

"She has a maid after all," Rosalind said, opening her fan and gently waving it in front of her face. "And she said she wanted to surprise us."

"Surprise? What surprise?" Cam asked. "I know what her gown looks like. I paid for it."

"My lords and ladies, if I may have your attention please?" Oakley's voice boomed out from the landing. He slowly walked to the top of the stairs, splendid in his brocade coat, and white stockings, his buckled shoes polished to a mirror's gleam. Incredibly, he carried a staff almost as long as he was tall. He descended the stairs with more than his customary regality, stopped before them and holding himself erect, struck the floor with his staff three times.

"I present to you, Lady Perdita Hunt," he announced solemnly. If not for the twinkle in his eyes, Oakley might have been presenting the Regent himself.

The soft rustle of a gown's hem along the parquet floor in the hall above them announced the appearance of the young lady in question. Slowly, carefully, Perdita came down the stairs, her gaze locked on Cam's face as if it were a beacon drawing her closer. She smiled shyly and tears pricked Cam's eyes. His little sister was a young lady.

Then as Perdita reached the last step, he stared long and hard at her.

Green. Her gown was pale green, not the pink she loved so much. Green with a lacy overskirt. Just like the one Amanda Fleming purchased. What the devil was going on?

"I say Perdy, we'll be beating the fellows back with Oakley's staff after you make your bow," Richard said.

"All the other debutantes will be wild with jealousy when they see you," Allister predicted. "By Jove, if   they   won't   be!"
 "It's lovely, Perdita," Gwenyth said softly, and Rosalind nodded.

Perdita curtsied and smiled the smile that always won her whatever she wanted. "Thank you," she said simply.

Cam swallowed the lump in his throat and said, "A private word with your oldest brother, Perdita?"

"Ah, now the advice begins," Richard teased as Cam took Perdita by the arm and gently led her toward the parlor.

"Don't dance with anyone more than twice—"

"Be sure to be demure, and always stay pure—" Allister recited.

Under the noise of their family's laughter, Cam closed the door and put his hands on Perdita's shoulders. "Dearest, what is going on? Where is your pink gown? Why are you wearing one that looks like Miss Fleming's?"

His sister's eyes filled with tears. "Because it *is* hers. Oh, Cam, Amanda gave me her gown!"

"What?"

Perdita nodded. " My dress arrived yesterday while you were gone and when I opened the box, there was an *orange* gown inside. I didn't know what to do, so I sent for Amanda to come over early and she said I must have *her* dress. She took me back to the rectory straightway and sent for Mrs. Nichols, who stayed up all night remaking Amanda's gown, so I could have it by tonight. You've always said I look well in pale green, almost as well as I do in pink, and there wasn't time to make up a pink one, or send to London for another one, so you *must* pay Mrs. Nichols a *huge* amount for helping me. Oh, Cam, Amanda gave me her gown! I do love her so much; she's become like a sister to me. You must find a way to thank her for helping me—oh Cam!" Perdita's voice broke. "*She gave me her gown!*"

Tears ran down Perdita's cheeks and Cam folded her into his arms. "Hush, darling," he whispered against her hair. "You look beautiful. You'd look beautiful in an old horse's blanket. Or a horse's old blanket. Or both."

She giggled and he took out his handkerchief to pat her cheeks. "You mustn't have red eyes for Winter Ball," he scolded.

"Red eyes would have clashed terribly with an orange gown," she said, and the smile he loved so well appeared.

"Terribly," he agreed, putting away his handkerchief. "And

yes, of course, I'll pay Mrs. Nichols and we'll find a way to thank Miss Fleming."

"Amanda," Perdita corrected. "You said you would call her Amanda when it was just us together."

"Amanda," he repeated. "But now, dearest—"he shot a quick glance at the clock on the mantle—"I think we best join the others in the hallway. It's nearly eight o'clock and our guests will arrive at any time."

"Except for the Henrys," she teased. "They're always late. It's their tradition."

"Always late," Cam agreed and they went to the foyer to join their family while with every step his heart beat in rhythm to the word, *Amanda. Amanda. Amanda.*

****

"Edward Guest, Viscount Pembroke, Lady Emmaline Guest, Viscountess Pembroke, The Honorable Lucy Guest," Oakley announced from the top of the stairs leading down to the ballroom.

Was it his imagination, or did the conversations of his surrounding guests in the nearly full ballroom die away? Descending the five steps, dressed in a gown of dazzling white, a coronet of white roses in her hair, Lucy looked every inch the aristocrat that she was. Beautiful. Posed. Polished. She was in every way, the perfect wife for an earl.

They stopped at the receiving line and Cam bowed. "Welcome to the Winter Ball," he said, speaking the formal words. "We are so glad you are able to join us."

"My lord, St. Cloud, the room is lovely," Lady Emmaline said. "Whose idea was it to decorate in silver and gold? The flowers are especially beautiful."

"It was all Perdita's idea," Cam answered. "I just pay the bills."

The Pembrokes laughed and Lady Emmaline said, "You should be proud of yourself, Perdita. Your mother would be."

"Perdita, you look lovely," Lucy said, opening her fan. "But I thought you told me your gown was pink."

"I changed my mind at the last minute," Perdita said as Richard and Allister chatted with Pembroke. "You look very pretty too, Lucy."

"So Richard is going to be your racer," Pembroke cut in. "Much competition this year, St. Cloud?"

"Against the St. Clouds?" Cam affected a haughty expression. "I think not."

"I hoped to see you race, Cameron," Lucy said. "Richard, can we not persuade you to let Cameron race instead?"

Richard imitated Cam's early expression. "Not race for the St. Clouds? I think not."

They all laughed but Cam's felt forced and he kept his gaze on Lucy, trying not to gaze at the top of the stairs and the appearance of a certain young lady. With supreme effort, he gave his attention back to Pembroke and his family.

"And who knows what the New Year will bring?" Lady Pembroke asked, looking directly at her host. "Changes, good fortune, Perdita's first Season, engagements—"

"The Reverend Mister Stephen Fleming and Miss Amanda Fleming," Oakley called.

The Pembrokes moved away to mingle with the other guests, and the conversations started up again. Cam struggled to keep his features impassive as he watched the Flemings descend the steps.

Stephen Fleming looked quite smart in his ensemble of black and white, and as at home here as in the pulpit. One would think he attended balls like this all the time.

Beside him, Amanda wore a simple, high-waisted gown of ivory with a matching silver ribbon under the bodice, complimenting her brother's attire. Among the wealth of silk and satin finery, her simplicity shimmered like a newly opened pearl, and she moved with the same confidence as her brother. Her gaze fixed on his, and Cam's heart turned over as he recalled how she had looked in the gown that Perdita now wore. By heaven, he would pay Mrs. Nichols three times the price of the gown for helping to make Perdita's night perfect.

But how in the world could he thank Amanda?

The Flemings stopped, and Cam introduced them to his brothers and their wives, and then watched in amazement as Amanda and Perdita exchanged compliments on their gowns. From their smiles and soft laughter, one would never suspect a near disaster had been averted. Thanks to Amanda.

Cam glanced at Oakley who tapped a gloved finger on the side of his nose to show that all the guests had arrived.

From the upstairs gallery, a waltz began, and as if by an unspoken signal, the guests stepped back to watch Cam put his arm around Perdita's waist and sweep her out onto the floor for the traditional opening dance.

"Do you suppose," he said, his heart nearly breaking with brotherly pride, "that the patronesses at Almack's will be upset for our waltzing in public before you make your bow?"

She wrinkled her nose in true Perdita fashion. "Silly old tabbies, trying to spoil people's fun. Besides, you're my brother, and this is *our* ball, so who will care? But I shan't tell if you don't."

"I'll take it to my grave," he said and her bright laughter rang out over the ballroom. No one, not his mother, not an army of governesses or even her finishing school teachers, had ever been able to quell Perdita's laugh.

And for that, Cam owed them a million thanks.

The waltz ended and after kissing her hands, the guests joined them on the floor. Cam spent the next half hour dancing with his sisters-in-law, and his other guests. Country dances, cotillion and even a reel. Between dances he discussed the upcoming race with the gentlemen and listened to the ladies swap the latest on-dits from London.

And all the while, Amanda seemed to keep her distance, managing not once to be in his set during the country dances. It was the hardest thing he had ever done not to seek her out with his eyes.

Another waltz began and he sought out Lucy. The other guests—as if to acknowledge their approval of the future uniting of the houses of Pembroke and St. Cloud—let them have the floor to themselves.

"When does your Aunt Adelaide arrive?" he asked. Her gloved hand in his was warm, her face held the usual serenity. Cam could not imagine this exquisite and perfectly-behaved creature ever riding neck or nothing, or arguing with the Vestry and their wives.

Or giving away a ball gown.

"Any time now," she said, smiling up at him. "We pray she'll be here by Christmas. It wouldn't be the same holiday without her."

"I hope you'll let me know the moment she arrives," Cam said.

She gave his hand a gentle squeeze. "The very moment. I promise."

The music ended and he led her back to her chair and her smiling mother. Another waltz began, and Cam made his way to stop before Amanda's chair and bow.

"Miss Fleming, if you are not otherwise engaged, I should like to dance with you."

The open fan she held began to beat a little faster, and her eyes lowered to stare at it. "Thank you, my lord, but—"

Cam bowed again. "I insist."

She raised her eyes and regarded him solemnly. Then she closed her fan, and stood to take his hand. He swept her out onto the crowded floor, maneuvering them close to the French doors that lead to the garden.

"I don't know how I can thank you." Cam saw no reason not to get to the point. "Perdita told me everything."

"She was so worried," his partner said softly. "Worried that she would embarrass you and your family by not looking well on this night of nights. Indeed, I think she would have gladly worn the orange gown at her court presentation rather than at her first Winter Ball. And so—"

"You gave her your gown," Cam interrupted. "There is not a single woman of my acquaintance who would have made such a sacrifice."

"It's not nearly so important that I look fashionable tonight, Cameron. I'm only a clergyman's sister; not a young woman preparing to enter Society."

Her self-deprecation nearly caused Cam to miss a step, and her hushed pronunciation of his name sent a wave of affection surging over him.

"I must disagree with that," he said at last. "I'm beginning to think you are one of the most amazing people I've ever met. Miss Fleming—Amanda—"

The waltz ended and she gave a quick curtsey, murmuring something about a headache before she hurried away. Cam stared after her but any plan to engage her once more was stopped by a gentle hand on his arm.

"I do think that tonight is already a success," Emmaline Guest was saying. "Oakley has just sent word to Lady Perdita that the buffet supper is ready. I've no doubt its richness will only add to the evening's enjoyment."

Knowing he could hardly refuse to dine at his own party, or not escort the highest-ranking lady present into the dining room, Cam forced his lips into a smile of acceptance. "Then let's go see what my kitchen staff prepared for us."

Chapter Sixteen

"I say, Amanda, it's not like you to go all faint and delicate—especially at a ball," Stephen said, as he stirred up the fire in the rectory library. "Did something happen between you and St. Cloud?"

They had asked Oakley to give their apologies to St. Cloud and Perdita, and returned to the rectory. Hamish slept in his basket, snoring softly. The only other sound was the crackle of the fire. Stephen put down the poker, turned, cocked his head, and watched her.

"Does this have something to do with you giving Perdita your gown?" he asked "And I must say again, even if you are my sister, I think that was the most unselfish thing I've ever known anyone to do. But you looked wonderful in that ivory gown."

"It wasn't the gown, Stephen."

"Then what? Was St. Cloud rude to you? Was anyone rude to you?"

The sorrow in Amanda's heart grew to an almost unbearable heaviness. "No," she said. "I mean, yes. I mean—oh Stephen, I've done it again. I've cost you your living here at All Souls."

Confusion and astonishment narrowed his eyes. "Mandy, what in the world are you talking about? Your behavior here has been blameless."

"People are talking about us," she choked. "Or they will.

And when that happens, then Perdita and Cameron's future prospects for marriage will be ruined."

"I don't understand." The tenderness in Stephen's voice nearly brought her to tears.

"Then sit down, please." Tension spread throughout Amanda's body, tightening her muscles into a painful coil as she watched him sit in the high-backed chair and stretch out his legs.

"I'm listening," he said.

She told him of the triumvirate's visit after his departure yesterday and their veiled threats and insinuations. "We can't let Cameron and Perdita be hurt by us, Stephen," she choked. "We must leave Huntingdown after Christmas."

"But we've done nothing wrong!" An unfamiliar anger laced his voice. "This is all nonsense!"

"But some people are angry at us, Stephen—especially the Triumvirate and their husbands. Or rather, at me. Perdita and St. Cloud don't deserve to be made unhappy by scandal or even idle gossip. And those women are just the ones to start it. Perdita hasn't even made her debut yet. I would never forgive myself if her chance for happiness was spoiled by my being even slightly indiscreet. And St. Cloud is only waiting for Lucy's great-aunt Adelaide to return before he proposes. Everyone at the ball said so. A scandal would ruin that too. Don't you see? We must leave Huntingdown after Christmas?"

"Does your being in love with St. Cloud have anything to do with this?"

His question jerked Amanda's gaze up from the carpet to his face. There was no sense trying to pretend she didn't understand his question or deny what he obviously knew. He was her twin and he knew her as well as she knew him, so she could only nod in miserable silence.

"I wouldn't want you to have a moment's sorrow, Mandy," Stephen said at last. "I'll write to Master Phillips the day after Christmas and tell him if he hasn't found someone for the position at Oxford I would like be considered. I'm sure he'll agree."

"Thank you." Amanda managed not to strangle on the words.

"There's one thing I don't understand, though," Stephen said, untying his elaborate cravat and tossing it aside. "It's not like you to give up without a fight. Why are you letting these women push you around?"

"I haven't anything to fight with," Amanda said. "St. Cloud and Lucy—"

"Oh, for heaven's sake, Mandy, call him Cameron. You're having a conversation with *me.*"

She bowed her head again. "I've never been in love, before," she said. "I don't think I could stand to stay and listen to you read out Cameron and Lucy's banns. It would break my heart."

"Ah, Mandy." Stephen rose and came to put his arms around her. His brotherly warmth spread around her and Amanda gave herself up to tears. She cried for a long time, listening to the slow, calm beating of his heart.

"Look, here's Hamish finally awake," Stephen said at last. "Did we remember to feed him before we left?" The Scottie had come to sit at their feet, his stubby tail moving back and forth on the carpet.

A hiccoughing laugh broke through the last of Amanda's sobs and she leaned down to pick up the little dog. "No," she said, "bad parents that we are."

Hamish barked in agreement, bringing the siblings to more laughter. "How can I be sad for long when I have a Scottie in my lap?" Amanda asked, rubbing Hamish's back.

"Not long," Stephen agreed, standing up to stretch out his long body, his arms over his head. "I suppose we should go to bed. After all, the sleigh race is tomorrow."

"And you'll win," Amanda declared, putting Hamish on the floor. "You'll even beat Richard Hunt, with that marvelous stepper Squire Beecham loaned you. I'd wager even money on it if it wouldn't cause even more scandal. It will show all of Huntingdown that if they are to be rid of us, your winning the annual race instead of a St. Cloud, will give them something to talk about it for years."

"Say that again." Stephen froze in mid-stretch.

"I said you'll even beat Richard Hunt and—"

"No. That other thing you said."

Amanda squinted up at him. "About giving Huntingdown something to talk about?"

A sly, most un-clergyman like smile crept across Stephen's face. "Yes. Exactly."

****

Early the next morning.
I'm terribly sorry, Lucy, but I can't marry you.

"No, that won't do." Cam stared at the penned words on the page, then squashed the paper and tossed it onto the floor. He had to be sure the words he spoke to Lucy were just right—if any words for breaking off a relationship could be right.

He rubbed his sleepless eyes, reached for another piece of paper, picked up his pen and started again. The quill's scratching was loud in the silence of his bedroom, drowning out the whispered tick of the wall clock.

Our families have always been friends, Lucy, and I know our fathers thought we'd be a good match, but. . .

"Damn!" Cam threw down his quill, shoved the single sheet along with a stack of paper aside, so that it drifted to the floor, and went to stand before the window. A lacy frost iced the windows and a new fallen snow covered the grounds as far as the eye could see. It should be a good day for the sleigh race.

But what about the rest of the day and the rest of his life? Cam leaned his forehead against the glass. There was no other course open to him but to try to explain to Lucy Guest that he could not, would not, marry her. It was as simple as that, if something like love could ever be simple. But there it was.

He was in love with Amanda Fleming. The realization lightened his heart and the weariness from the previous sleepless night, spent staring into the dark, left him. He was in love with Amanda Fleming.

His brain sent out a howl of protest. *Have you lost your mind? No breath of scandal has ever touched the St. Clouds. And you're going to be the first? What about tradition and honor and dignity and keeping your word? What about the St. Cloud name?*

But you, Cameron Hunt, never gave any promise, his heart countered. *You just went along because your father suggested it would be a good idea to marry Lucy and you knew her and like her. But* you *never gave your word or your promise.*

And then incredibly, he heard his mother's beloved voice whisper in his brain. A voice that had been as much a part of raising him as his father's. A voice he had loved just as much.

Listen to your heart, my son. Listen to your heart.

Damnation, why was he waiting? He sprang for the bell- pull, yanked it several times, then hurled himself into his dressing room and started grabbing blindly at his clothing. What did a man wear on such an occasion? Where the devil were Oakley and Higgens?

He jerked the dressing room's bell pull, and grabbing several suits from the rack, carried them back to the bedroom and threw them on the bed before lighting more candles and stirring up the fire.

"Shoes or boots?" he muttered, returning to the dressing room to gather up an armload of both. Halfway across the room, his bare foot slid over a stray sheet of paper He opened his arms to steady himself and his foot ware fell to the floor, scattering around the carpet. He stumbled on to the bureau, yanked open the drawer and began to paw through his linen, undoing Higgens's neat stacks.

"Neck-cloth. Simple or elaborate?" Can asked the room. When several of those were collected and scattered on his desk like so many discarded sheets of paper, he went to stand in front of the full-length mirror in the corner and raked his hands through his hair. Should he let Higgens trim it a bit? No, wait. His valet did it only two days ago. And would there be time for a bath? No, just a quick scrub-up at the washstand and where the devil were his servants? "Oakley! Higgens!"

"You rang, my lord?"

Cam spun on his heel to find both men behind him, their eyes wide with surprise and shock as they took in the avalanche of disordered clothing and their equally disordered employer. Of course they would be shocked. Cam had never raised his voice to them, much less thrown his clothing around the room.

But then today was going to be a day like no other day.

"Oakley, wake George," Cam ordered, walking to the bed. "Tell him to get my smaller carriage ready to go to the Pembrokes as soon as possible."

"Th-the P-Pembrokes?" Oakley stuttered. He glanced at the wall clock and looked back at Cam. "But it's five o'clock in the morning, sir."

"I can tell time, Oakley!" Cam shouted. Then a tiny bit of reason entered his brain. "Sorry. Just tell him to do it, please. I won't need Quinn. Then bring me a cup of very strong tea. I've no doubt Cook is already preparing the post-race breakfast. Hurry, man!"

"Yes sir." Oakley nearly fled from the room.

"Higgens, which of those suits do you think would be suitable?" Cam took his valet by the arm and dragged the man to the bed. "I've half a dozen here and I can't decide."

"For an early morning call, my lord?" The usual placid calm had returned to Higgens's face. He studied the array of clothing with narrowed eyes and frowned

175

thoughtfully. "I would say the black with the golden waistcoat. Shoes, not boots."

"Black, golden waistcoat, shoes," Cam agreed, like a child reciting a lesson. "Good. Very good."

"Very good, my lord," Higgens repeated. "As to your neck-cloth, sir, might I suggest something simple but elegant?"

"By heaven, of course. Brilliant!" Cam praised. "Remind me to raise your salary, Higgens."

"Thank you, my lord," Higgens said, as he began to gather up the other clothing. "Ah…my lord?"

"Yes?"

"May I be the first to wish you joy? I have no doubt that Lady Lucy will make a splendid countess and you will know every happiness."

Oakley returned with a tray bearing a jug of hot water and the requested cup of tea. He poured the water into the washbasin, handed Cam the cup and asked, "Is there a note you would like George to deliver to the Pembrokes before you call on them, my lord?"

"No, thank you."

"But isn't that rather untraditional, my lord?" Oakley exchanged glances with Higgens. "Given the hour?"

By heaven, it's only the first tradition I'm going to be breaking today. "The element of surprise has its advantages, Oakley. Especially where women are concerned."

"I see," Oakley said, and this time he and Higgens exchanged smiles and nods of understanding. "Will you announce the first banns this Sunday?"

"I hope so," Cam said. "I sincerely hope so."

"My lord?" Higgens said. "I know you always shave yourself, but just this once, would you let me do the honors? We wouldn't want your hands…ah…how should I put this? In your excitement—"

"Anticipation," Oakley corrected, rocking back on his heels.

Higgens snapped his fingers in agreement. "Much better. We wouldn't want your anticipation of the morning's upcoming events to unsteady your hands."

Would my hands really tremble so much? Gratefully, Cam drank his tea, handed Oakley the cup and said, "Yes, thank you, Higgens. I would appreciate that."

And as Cam sat down for the most important shave of his life, he listened to the joyful beating of his heart. *Amanda. Amanda. Amanda.*

****

Lights blazed from every window in the Pembrokes's home, and apprehension tightened Cam's body into pulsing knots as his carriage made its way up the long drive. It was well-known among the ton that the Pembrokes were notoriously late sleepers, seldom rising before ten o'clock in the morning, and yet it appeared that everyone was up and awake at the unspeakably early hour of six. Something had happened.

Aunt Adelaide has arrived. It was the only answer. Trying to ignore the furious knocking of his heart, Cam brushed the front of his coat, took off his hat to smooth his hair and filled his lungs with air. His long, slow exhalation brought no relief, but rather increased his sense of foreboding.

George pulled the horses to a stop, but before he could move off his perch, Cam got out of the carriage and took the steps up to the porch two at a time. At the top, the door swung open and Franklin, the Pembrokes's butler ushered him inside.

"Lord St. Cloud," he said, making a hasty bow. "We were just about to send for you."

Cam cocked his head towards the sweeping staircase as he gave the servant his coat and hat. A faint wailing followed by a more distinct bellow sounded from the second floor. "Is something wrong?"

"I think it best for Lady Lucy to tell you herself, my lord," Franklin said. "If you will just excuse me, I will announce you."

The servant's speedy gait as he headed in the direction of the conservatory only added to Cam's uneasiness. Butlers didn't move that fast unless the house was on fire. But soon Franklin returned, his features tight with worry.

"If you will come with me, my lord." Franklin took off again, and Cam followed. They stopped by an open door and Franklin stepped back to allow Cam to enter. Lucy rose from a long sofa near the fire, her expression composed and serene, as if she expected him. "Good morning, Cameron," she said.

He bowed. "Good morning, Lucy. Forgive my calling so early and without an invitation, but there is something I must say to you."

"And I to you."

Ignoring every good manner he possessed that would have allowed her to speak first, Cam said, "Lucy, I know this is going to be hard for you to hear, and I hope you know I would never hurt you, but I can't marry you. I can't."

Lucy's eyes widened. "You can't?"

"No." Cam spread his hands. "I don't love you, so how can I possibly marry you?"

"You don't love me?"

"No. I'm sorry."

Her lips tightened, then began to tremble, and then she let out a whoop of laughter that would have done Perdita proud. She clapped a hand over her mouth, but it was useless. She continued to laugh and laugh until Cam began to think she was having hysterics. "Lucy, I'm sorry—"

"But that's wonderful, Cameron! Simply wonderful!" she gasped, pulling out a handkerchief to wipe her eyes.

Cam blinked. "It is?"

"Yes, of course! Because you see, I don't love you either."

"You don't?"

"No. I mean I like you, I'm fond of you—"

"As I am fond of you—"

"But it would never have worked anyway," Lucy said through hiccups of laughter. "Because you see, I'm already married."

"Married?" Cam choked on the word. *"Married?"*

"For three years." Her laughter having finally subsided, she went to the French doors that lead out to the garden and called, "You can both come in now."

"About time! I thought we were going to freeze to death out there!" The unmistakable figure of Adelaide Cheswick, Dowager Duchess of Clairfield strode in, stamping the snow from her boots. Countless debutants had trembled under her scrutiny, and her approval was nearly as important as that of the patronesses of Almack's. But today she was smiling, obviously very pleased with not only herself, but with the situation unfolding. She came forward to shake Cam's hand with a firm grip. "Good morning, St. Cloud."

"Your Grace." Cam bowed. "I trust I find you well?"

"For someone of my age who's spent all night traveling just to get here in time for the race, I'm well enough. Damn snow slowed us down, but we're finally here in one piece. Lucy dear, do get on with it. St. Cloud looks as if he might fall over from shock."

Lucy gestured at the silent young man in travel-stained clothing who entered behind the duchess. He slipped his arm around Lucy's waist and kissed her on the cheek. "So this is the fellow your parents wanted you to marry?"

Lucy smiled at him. "It is. Cameron, this is my husband, Benjamin Hampson, just arrived from India. Benjamin, this is Cameron Hunt, the ninth earl of St. Cloud."

Cam bowed again. "Mr. Hampson. Did Her Grace bring you?"

"She did," Hampson said cheerfully, bowing as well as he could with one arm still around Lucy. "Pleased to meet you, my lord. I suppose an explanation is in order."

"If you wouldn't mind," Cam said.

"A simple one, then. Lucy and I met shortly after her eighteenth birthday. It was love at first sight."

"He's so romantic," Lucy sighed. "I knew at that moment that Benjamin was the only man for me."

"As a third son, I had no money to call my own," Hampson continued. "I had to make my own way. We married secretly by special license just before I set out for India. I swore to Lucy that after three years I would return either rich, or just as poor as when I left. I didn't want to just take her money, you see, knowing she would inherit a pile of it from her Aunt Addy when she turned twenty-one."

The duchess beamed at them. "Aunt Addy. That's me."

"Ah, yes. Of course." Relief and understanding surged through Cam. "That's why you insisted on attending that three-year finishing school," he said. "It was a smokescreen to cover your marriage. As long as you were at school, your parents wouldn't insist you marry."

"Didn't I tell you Cam was clever, Benjamin?" Lucy asked proudly. She might have been describing the feats of an older brother. "Aunt Addy was in on our secret as was my school friend, Ruth. She has a brother in India and Benjamin would put his letters to me in with hers. We didn't want Mama and Papa to find out. I'm sorry to have deceived you for so long, but—"

Suddenly light-headed, Cam waved away her words. "Nothing to be sorry for, Lucy. There was only an expectation, not a promise made. And since bigamy is illegal in England and I cannot condone adultery, of course we can't marry."

The others laughed and Lucy said, "I'm so glad that you understand Cam. And I'm so glad that you don't love me!"

"Trust me, I do understand." Cam turned his head toward the open door. The faint wailing could still be heard, and he added, "But I don't think your parents will."

"They'll adjust when they see the size of Benjamin's bank account," the duchess said with a wink. "The lad has made a *fortune*."

Cam took Lucy's hands and bowed. "May I be the first as an old family friend to wish you complete joy," he said. "If you will excuse me, I need to help Richard prepare for the race."

And then Cameron Hunt, ninth earl of St. Cloud, a man known

for his unswerving calm and complete dignity in public, ran from the room.

Chapter Sixteen

"Where is Fleming?" Richard asked, blowing on his gloved hands. "Everyone else is here."

The temperature had fallen to below freezing the night before, and a wind ruffled the standards on the waiting sleighs. The horses stomped and tossed their heads as if they understood why they were there. A late December sun, while providing very little warmth, poured out a brilliant light.

But the cold had not prevented hundreds of spectators, bundled to the eyes, from gathering at Heart's Ease. Green and white flags staked to the ground, lined the two-mile stretch.

"He has only five minutes before starting time," Allister said, rubbing the neck of Charming, Richard's horse. "Cam, do you think should we should send for him?"

I'll have plenty to say to him when he gets here. Cam shook his head. "He'll come."

"There he is!" Perdita said, pointing at a rapidly approaching bright red Tilbury sleigh. She waved and called, "Hello, Stephen!"

The sleigh stopped and the seated figure nodded. A long scarf wrapped several times around his neck covered the lower part of his face, showing only his eyes. A tall hat perched on his head and he nodded. "'Morning, Lady Perdita," he said gruffly, the scarf muffling his voice. "'Morning, my lord."

"You're late," Cam said sternly. "The race is about to start."

Fleming shrugged. "Sorry. Couldn't find my lucky hat."

"Where's Amanda?" Perdita asked. "Isn't she coming?"

"She's around somewhere."

Squire Beecham, master of ceremonies, shouldered his way among them. "Glad to see ye, Mr. Fleming, glad to see ye," he greeted. "If you and Mr. Richard will just take your place among the others, we'll start."

Fleming nodded, clucked to his horse and they moved toward the waiting line of sleighs. Richard kissed Gwenyth, climbed into his sleigh and drove off. Cam looked at his family and asked, "Shall we go to our seats?" The Hunts traditionally sat on a reviewing stand to watch the race.

"I'm staying right here," Gwenyth said firmly. "I want to be as close to Richard as possible when he wins."

"Me too," Rosalind said.

"I'm staying here," Perdita announced.

"Have it your way," Cam growled. "Allister, are you coming?"

Allister laughed. "And anger my wife? You have a lot to learn about women, Cam."

Cam strode away, trying not to be too obvious in his scanning of the crowd for Amanda Fleming. But with everyone in face-covering scarves and hats, it was impossible to spot her. He climbed into the St. Cloud's reviewing stand and sat.

He should have gone to the church after leaving Lucy to speak with Amanda. Tell her what had happened. Tell her he loved her. Ask her to marry him, if she would have him.

But as tradition dictated, the kitchen staff at Heart Ease had prepared a special early breakfast for the Hunts, and Cam would not hurt their feelings by arriving late and missing it. He'd already skirted close enough to scandal this morning. Unfortunately, Amanda—darling Amanda—would have to wait.

The starting pistol cracked and Cam stood as the crowd began to shout. The seven sleighs sped across the hard ground, the drivers whistling and calling encouragement to their horses, the sleigh's standards whipping like leaves against a whirlwind. Cam followed the progress of Richard's bright blue sleigh, easily pulling ahead of the others. Richard was an excellent whip, and Cam had no doubt he would regain the prize for the St. Clouds.

But Fleming was right with him, passing the others with considerable skill. If not for his brother's entering the race, Cam would have cheered for the clergyman, whose arrival in Huntingdown had done so much already for the village.

As had his sister's. Cam shifted his attention from the racers just long enough to scan the crowd again. As Richard and Fleming neared the halfway point, the crowd's shouts became a roar, and Cam leaned forward. Fleming and Richard were side by side, and excitement told hold of him. "Go, Richard!" he shouted, getting to his feet. "Drive that pony!"

"Good morning, my lord. Nice day for a one horse open sleigh race, isn't it?"

A man's pulpit-trained voice jerked Cam around and he found himself face to face with Stephen Fleming. His long scarf was wrapped around not his face, but his neck and he wore not a tall hat, but the traditional one of a country clergyman.

"Fleming?" Cam croaked. "But if you're here, then who the devil is in——." He squinted at the red sleigh and its driver, having passed the half-way mark and was hurtling closer and closer to the finish line. "*No*. It can't be. *Amanda?*"

"Fooled you, didn't she?" Triumphant rage simmered in Fleming's usually mild eyes. "We've done it before at a masked dress ball, dressed alike, and no one was the wiser. Being twins we were able to carry it off. We thought it would be a nice farewell touch since we're being forced to leave Huntingdown."

Lack of sleep and Lucy's news had stretched Cam's nerves to the breaking point. "Forced to leave? Fleming, what the hell are you talking about?"

Fleming's stare was just short of contempt. "You really don't know, do you, St. Cloud? About the triumvirate?"

"Know what about whom?" Cam shouted.

Fleming told him. Told him everything. "Amanda and I can't possibly stay with both you and Perdita's reputation at stake," he concluded. "Amanda loves you, you silly clod. She loves Perdita as well. We're leaving after the New Year for me to take up a teaching post at Oxford so you can marry Lucy Pembroke without scandal and Perdita can make a good marriage."

"Like hell you're leaving," Cam bit off. "Fleming, I—."

The crowd's noise forced his attention back to the race and the final approach of two sleighs. Charming, Richard's sleek black horse hovered on the verge of taking the lead, and Cam thought he heard his family cheering and chanting, "St. Cloud! St. Cloud! St. Cloud!"

But then the red Tilbury burst ahead, and a gust of wind blew up, knocking off the driver's tall hat. A mass of golden hair tumbled down, and Cameron Hunt's heart was forever captured as Amanda Fleming's sleigh surged forward over the finishing line to victory.

The crowd's shouts became howls and screams of surprise, outrage or outright laughter. Amanda pulled her horse to a stop, and Cam saw a small black head rising from underneath a blanket on the floorboard. It might have been madness or joy, but Cam could swear Hamish's gaze locked on his face and once again, winked at him.

A fit of laughter seized Cam and he jumped from the dais, his boots hitting the frozen ground. He stumbled, but regained his footing and straightened his coat.

"Fleming," he shouted over his shoulder as he bolted for the finishing line. "Don't go anywhere. I've something important to ask you."

He shoved his way through the people crowding around Amanda's sleigh, most of them applauding. Richard's sleigh was beside hers, and to Cam's immense relief, his brother was laughing.

"By Jove," he gasped, "that's the best piece of racing I've seen in years! Where did you learn to handle a horse like that?"

"This is outrageous!" Tarwater shouted. "A woman racing? Women aren't allowed to race."

"There's nothing in the rules that says a woman can't race," Amanda shouted back, brushing aside her curls. "It says, 'the racer must be of good character and have the necessary skills.' And I have both."

"It's disgraceful!" Tarwater's voice became a bellow. "*You're* disgraceful, and we're well rid of you and your brother!"

He reached up as if to grab Amanda out of the sleigh, but Cam seized his shoulder and spun him around. "I'll ask you not to speak to my future countess that way, Tarwater," he warned. "And since I can't hit your wife for making Amanda's life miserable these past few weeks, you'll do quite nicely."

With one well-placed punch, Cam's fist put Tarwater on the ground, clutching his nose. Glaring at the shock-silenced crowd, and finding more guilty parties, Cam asked, "Baker? Hopewell? Your wives are just as much a part of this. Do I need to redesign your noses as well?"

"N-no, my lord," Baker stuttered. An ashen-faced Hopewell only nodded, shock muting any protest he might make.

"Good." Cam directed his gaze at the crowd again. "Anyone else?"

When no answer came, he turned and held up his hand to Amanda. "Dearest," he said, not giving a damn who heard him, or that his voice was on the point of breaking. "Would you allow me to help you down?"

For a long moment, Amanda stared at him and the hope in Cam's heart threatened to turn to despair. Silence spread out over the crowd, as if they, like Cam were holding their breath.

Then Hamish barked, breaking the silence, and Amanda laughed. Giving Cam her hand, she let him lift her over the side of the Tilbury to stand beside him.

"I suppose I should wait and do this privately," he said in a voice that carried out over the heads of the spectators. "Or at least until I've spoken to your brother. But I will have no rumors or talk about us. Amanda Fleming, I love you with all my heart. Will you marry me?"

A love he prayed he would deserve answered in her eyes, giving them a brilliance that was almost blinding. She placed her beloved hands on either side of his face. "Of course," she said in a much softer voice. "Of course."

"I've never kissed a woman wearing trousers before," he said. "But since today seems to be about breaking traditions, I might as well add another of my own."

"Oh, Cam, this is marvelous!" Perdita said. "Amanda and I are going to be sisters?"

"Hush, Perdita." Cam pulled Amanda into his arms to kiss her most thoroughly and the crowd erupted into wild applause. Her scent, one of flowers and summer days, filled his head and if not for her embrace, he would have floated right up to the heavens from happiness.

"Lucy's married," he whispered under the continuing applause, guessing she'd want to know. "Her husband of three years arrived this morning from India along with Aunt Adelaide."

She pulled back. "Really? Are you sure?"

"Met the fellow myself this morning," he said. "I'll tell you all about it once we're back at Heart's Ease."

"Will someone *please* let me through?" A slightly disheveled Stephen Fleming was pushing his way through the crowd. The applause stopped and silence swept over the crowd again as he stopped in front of Amanda and Cam.

"Well, my lord St. Cloud," he said, putting his hands on his hips. "I'll give you full points for bravado. A public proposal *and* a kiss indeed."

"I do have your permission, don't I?" Cam asked.

"You better say yes, Stephen," Amanda warned. "After all, I know all your secrets."

"Not all of them." A smile better suited to a rake than a clergyman crossed Fleming's face. "My lord, you said something earlier about having something important to ask me? Well, I need to ask you something as well. May we go somewhere private?"

****

The Next Day.

"It's a bit untraditional to do this on Christmas Eve, but I'm told the past twenty-four hours in Huntingdown have been vastly untraditional." The Reverend George Winterson, vested for the holiday, stood behind the pulpit and beamed at the packed church of All Souls. "I'm very glad Stephen invited me to spend the Christmas holidays with him and his sister or I would have missed this."

The congregation laughed and Winterson added, "I don't think he expected any of this when he issued that invitation, but I wouldn't have missed it for the world."

He cleared his throat and adopted a clergyman's solemn tone. "It is my great privilege to announce the first marriage banns not only between Miss Amanda Fleming and Cameron Hunt, the ninth Earl of St. Cloud, but also those of Lady Perdita Hunt and Mr. Stephen Fleming.If there be any impediment to these unions, I charge ye here in the name of heaven to name and declare it now."

In the following silence, and half expecting the triumvirate to try to get in one last word, Amanda's heart hammered so hard it hurt to breathe. But the warmth of Cam's hand in hers acted like a balm, soothing her fears and she turned to smile at him. His solemn expression was suitable for church, but his eyes twinkled with loving approval. "Happy?" he whispered, kissing her cheek.

"Only my wedding day will make me happier," she said.

"Soon, my love," he whispered again, squeezing her hand. "Very, very soon."

"Well, since there are no objections," Winterson said, "Stephen, come up here so we can start the service.

That is, after you've taken your fiancée to her place in the choir."

From across the aisle, a vested Stephen rose and led Perdita toward the front of the church. But then she whirled around, love and excitement lighting up her face.

"I say, Cam!" she cried. "Didn't I tell you this was going to be a cracking good Christmas?"

The congregation laughed again, and a grinning Stephen called out, "Wives! Whatever will we do with them?"

"Love them!" Cam shouted back as the music started and the choir filed in. "And have a cracking good time!"

One Horse Open Sleigh Race

ABOUT THE AUTHOR
A lifelong Anglophile, Karen Hall
makes her home in East Tennessee with Buddy and Febe the
WonderDogs. When not
writing romantic fiction, she loves singing in her church choir,
cooking for friends, and
trying to keep the weeds from taking over the flowerbeds

NOTE FROM AUTHOR
A percentage of the profits from the sale of this book starting with
the date of its release until December 31st 2013 will go to At Risk
Intervention, a non-profit organization in East Tennessee dedicated
to the rescue, treatment and placement of unwanted, neglected and
abused dogs.

Made in the USA
Coppell, TX
25 October 2022

85270613R10118